The Red Shoes

The Red Shoes

Amethyst Bercher

Marlena Wolf

Sapphyre Blue

Bradbury Stone

Candice Bradford

Our boundless thanks to Alex, without whom we would spend more time making our own cups of tea and less time writing.

Dear Reader,
Thank you for choosing to spend some time with a Wolfstone book.

We do hope you enjoy reading it as much as we enjoyed writing it.

Why not visit our web-page? www.wolfstone.com.au for links to our social media, our contact form or to tell us you have spotted a typo.
While you're there you can join our mailing list to be kept up to date with all the latest news and new releases.

We love to hear from our fans so don't be shy. Tell us what you like so we can give you more!

Rather wait until the end of the book to see if you like us? No problem we will put the details there too, just for you xx

Contents

Little Red Ride

She shimmied out of her sweat soaked clothes and threw herself onto the bed, still panting from her morning workout. She felt good, her blood was pumping, and she felt alive. Her skin glowed with tiny beads of moisture, and as she cooled down, her nipples became hard and started to ache. She reached up to play with them, taking each one between her thumb and middle finger and twisting it gently back and forth. She liked that; it sent an electric spark to her groin, and she felt herself growing warm and wet.

She reached one hand down between her legs to touch herself. She was wet and very aroused, as she often was after exercise, and was becoming more so, as she dipped her fingers into herself and played in her juices.

She reached into her bedside drawer and pulled out her new toy, grinning at the gentle purring sound it made when she turned it on. She slid it over her nipples first, then traced it down her body, enjoying the buzz along her skin. When she finally pressed it between her legs and then deep inside herself, she gasped out loud. She hadn't had this toy for very long, but she was enjoying it.

The gentle curve meant she could easily reach her g-spot and the little vibrating nub was in just the right position to press onto her clit. It was fabulous and well worth the money she had spent on it.

She laid back, her legs slightly bent, and plunged the toy deep into herself as she reached her first orgasm. She had heard that some women had trouble climaxing, but she never had. At least not when she was with a competent lover.

She smiled to herself at the thought of being her own competent lover. She was mostly fine with that, but there were moments when it would be nice to have a man that knew how to please her. It had been a long time. As she recalled past lovers, she moved so that the vibrations were getting her in just the right spot to get her over the line a second time.

She took a short breather and enjoyed the sensation of touching her now sensitive clit with her fingertips, then she turned up the power on her toy and slid it up inside herself again. This time she meant business and she pressed her hips up to meet her hand with each plunge of the toy as if she was moving to meet a thrusting lover while pinching and twisting her nipples with her free hand.

The sweat on her skin increased and she panted and grunted as she fucked herself to an amazing high and then groaned as she hit her next orgasm like a high-speed collision. She managed to switch off the vibrations just before she was spun into a centrifuge of pleasure and release.

She laid there panting and smiling and feeling good about her morning. She basked in the warm glow for a while, then got up and headed for the shower. She did have a job on today after all, so she had better start preparing.

She loved her new shower head; it had different settings that suited different things. She washed and rinsed her hair, shaved her legs and underarms; then turned to a high massage setting that stung as it hit her skin and made her tingle all over. It was always better when she had just had sex and her nipples were still sensitive. It felt like tiny needles piercing her skin and it made her feel alive. The tingle lasted long after she and her hair were dry.

She stood in front of the mirror admiring the pink glowing skin of her naked form. *Nice*, she thought, and smiled at her vanity as she moved back and forth to strike different poses. She ran her fingertips up the outside of her thigh and hip, then across her stomach and up to her breasts. She cupped one in her hand and felt the weight of it appreciatively. Not the small perky breasts of her youth she mused as she gently tweaked one still stinging nipple. Fuller, more mature but still firm. The sort of breasts that drove her clients wild when spilling over the top of a tightly laced corset as she administered whatever punishment was on the agenda for the day.

But no corset today. She wasn't even going into the 'office'. She would let the girls handle the heavy work for the day; she had a special assignment. She had been in the business ten years now and was starting to wind down her 'hands-on' dungeon work, with a view to retirement - or at least semi-retirement. She turned to admire the rear view and ran her hand over one well-rounded cheek, then broke her own reverie with a short, sharp slap.

She had her clothes laid out on the bed. Her grey, figure-hugging, woollen skirt, that came to just below the knee with a matching jacket and a plain white shirt. Very school ma'am-ish, she thought. Today, she was going for a slightly vampish headmistress look so she had also laid out fine net stockings with black lace tops that held snuggly to her thighs and a bright red bra with matching knickers edged in black and red lace.

Earlier, she'd sent the client a photo of the knickers with the promise that she would post them to him if he was a good boy and followed the rules. The finishing touch was her brand new bright red stilettos with the shiny black heels. She bought them on a whim from an odd little shop in Copenhagen when she was on holiday and had been aching for a chance to wear them.

She remembered the man who sold them to her. He looked about a million years old, but he fixed her with a steely eye and warned her that they were 'magic shoes'. "Not for the faint-hearted," he'd told her. She laughed at the memory.

Interesting sales technique she had thought at the time, and now today was the day to wear them.

She dressed with care, leaving just enough shirt buttons undone to give a tantalising glimpse of cleavage and lace and drew her hair back into a rather stern bun. Her makeup was subtle and understated with the exception of her lipstick, which was bright red to match her manicured fingernails, her underwear, and those gorgeous red shoes.

As she stepped her stockinged feet into the stilettos, she felt a rush of excitement race from her toes to her newly aroused pussy and decided she might enjoy just a little more play before she went to work. This time she stood leaning up against the wall in front of the mirror so that she could see the shoes.

She slid her fingers under the lace beneath her skirt and moved the crotch of her knickers to one side and found her swollen clit with her fingertips. She imagined a different *competent* lover. One that liked what she liked and knew how to turn her on and, more importantly, how to get her off. A strong, successful man who she could rely on but who would submit to her totally where and when it counted.

She thought about how he might smell, how he might feel, and even how he might taste, and it didn't take her long to make her own knees tremble as she climaxed for a fourth time that day.

She straightened herself up in front of the mirror and became aware that her underwear was now soaking wet. She smiled at the thought, knowing the client wouldn't mind at all.

She had sent him a message telling him which bus to be on, where to stand, and asked what he would be wearing so that she would recognise him. Despite all of that, she felt almost sure he wouldn't show as she stood at the bus stop. She checked her phone, half expecting a message to say he had changed his mind and had chickened out at the last minute, but there was nothing. So, she turned the phone off and put it in her jacket pocket. *Oh well*, she thought. He had already paid so it was no skin off her nose if she got all dressed up for nothing more than a short bus ride.

She stepped up onto the bus. She felt sexy and still quite aroused walking down the aisle in her new shoes and attracted quite a few admiring glances. He had been told not to make eye contact and he didn't, so she had plenty of opportunity to check him out as she walked towards him. Taller than she expected and better dressed. She knew he would be wearing black pants and a blue shirt, and she had instructed him to carry a black jacket or coat over his arm, so what he was wearing was no surprise, but she thought it was better quality than she expected and fitted him well.

He was standing where he had been told, holding the top rail with one hand and had his jacket draped over his other arm. She stood with her back to him and held the handle at the edge of a seat. As the bus pulled away from the kerb, it went over a speed hump and she took a small stumbling step back which *accidentally* brought one of her stiletto heels down on his foot. She thought she heard a barely perceptible groan, but he made no other sound. He had been warned if he made any noise she would get off the bus. So far, he was being very compliant, as she expected.

The next stop was outside a sporting field and a large number of young men got on the bus for the ride back from school sport, as she knew they would. This meant the aisle became very crowded and she was virtually pushed up against her client. Her heel was still on his foot, and now her backside was pressed firmly against him.

He felt good behind her, solid and strong. As the bus continued to fill they were bumped and jostled, and she felt him turn, slightly, so that she was pressing directly on the front of him. She pressed back harder and could feel him becoming erect as the movement of the bus caused her to rock and rub on him while still standing on his foot. Soon her backside was pressed hard up against an enormous erection.

Luckily, she had told him to bring the jacket; if she had to move for any reason he would have to cover himself for sure. No way would that monster go un-noticed, and she had no desire to be thrown off the bus.

On these 'special' expeditions she usually didn't have much desire of any sort, other than perhaps to get it over with and go home. For her, the pleasure usually lay in the meticulous planning rather than the execution of the act itself. She enjoyed developing the plan, setting the rules and sending the instructions, selecting what to wear and teasing the client with photographs of the underwear they may get to own if they behaved. This was a relatively new part of the plan, made necessary by one client that followed her, despite the rules to the contrary. So now there was an incentive for them to continue to comply with the instructions, even once the game was over.

Today was different, maybe because she was already hot and wet before she even left home or maybe because this guy was not what she expected but whatever the reason today she was truly enjoying rubbing herself on this strange man's cock. Just the thought of it was sending thrilling tingles to all the right places and turning her on in ways she hadn't been in a very long time.

The bus turned onto the cobblestoned mall section of the journey, as she knew it would, and the shuddering vibrations of the bus were going straight up her legs to her aching wet pussy and making her so hot she almost forgot why she was there, until she was jostled and pressed harder on to her client. She felt him moan but didn't hear a thing over the noise in the bus.

She was beginning to realise she might actually climax…in fact, she needed to. She was so hot that if she didn't orgasm soon she thought she might scream. The bus stopped to pick up more people and as it took off again, she found herself pressed tightly against him. So tightly she could feel his rapid breathing and his heart beating hard against his chest. She could even smell him, and it just made her wetter.

He smelled fresh and clean but masculine and with an odour of new sweat, undoubtedly from his present predicament. She almost wanted to turn around, but she was there in a professional capacity and forced herself to try to remember that. She really couldn't recall the last time she was so turned on by a client, if ever. She could feel her juices running down her thighs and soaking the tops of her stockings.

The bus moved onto the roadworks, as planned, and was forced to take some very tight turns, meaning she was rubbing side to side on the client's enormous cock and it was pulling her wet knickers across her clit. She was on the edge of exploding when the bus moved back out into the open road. She could feel him panting and realised she was starting to sweat too at the realisation that if either of them was going to climax it had to be soon. The bus would practically empty once it got to the school.

They went over a speed hump and she almost gasped. They hit a pothole and she had to bite her lip to not make a noise. Then they headed down a hill and over some more roadwork corrugations. She pressed herself on him so hard he had to re-adjust his grip as the vibrations and the rubbing and the wet lace of her knickers all worked together to grant her the enormous orgasm she was aching for.

Her knees went momentarily weak and she felt the client touch her lightly on the waist as if to steady her. Such a touch would normally end proceedings, but under the circumstances she let it go. She wasn't sure she could have walked the length of the bus at that moment anyway.

It only took her a few seconds to regain her composure and put her weight squarely on the stranger's foot and press down hard. She felt his cock twitch between her cheeks and she smiled to herself. She needed to get this guy off, she had to - he had earned it, and she was so grateful she had his phone number because she was sure she wanted to meet him again. She thought she might put a discount offer in with the knickers when she sent them. That made her smile.

She was brought back to herself when the bus braked and changed lanes. She realised she had only a few minutes before they would be at the school and she suddenly decided to break the rules herself.

She put her hand around behind her back, grabbed the rock-hard cock that was pressing into her and began to expertly jerk it off, through his trousers. The client wisely moved his jacket to give some cover although she knew that the couple in the seat beside them had cottoned on to what was happening and were watching eagerly. She could also feel other eyes were on her, but she didn't care. The knowledge that people were aware and watching just made it hotter.

His cock felt so good in her hand. She found herself imagining how good it would feel inside her and her heart began to race. Her juices soaked her knickers and her stockings and again, she didn't care. As they were approaching the school she could smell his sweat stronger and she was sure he knew it was all about to end. She worked his cock behind her back with expert strokes and knew he was close. She suddenly realised she was too.

The bus slowed to go over the speed humps leading up to the school; one, two of them and as they crested the third hump she felt him twitching and pulsing in her hand, so she knew he was climaxing and blowing his load in his pants just the way she wanted him to. As the back wheels hit the last hump, she was practically overcome by an orgasm that started in her toes and smashed over her entire body in wave after wave of pleasure. She rested her head momentarily on the stranger's chest and felt his large, powerful hand on her waist to steady her. Far from being upset by that, she was grateful for his strength.

As the bus parked outside the school, she felt him shuffle a little behind her, undoubtedly to cover up the mess he just made. She grinned a triumphant grin and moved with the disembarking crowd to exit the bus. She could feel his eyes on the back of her, boring into her like hot coals and she shuddered at the feel of it.

She didn't look back. It took all her strength and composure not to, but she didn't look back. She had his details on her phone, so everything would be okay. She hailed a taxi as the bus pulled away and as she headed for home, she pulled her phone out of her pocket to save his number.

As she turned the phone on, there was a barrage of messages, all from the client. *Eager* she thought to herself, given that he had only just moved off in the bus. But when she opened them, they were all pretty much the same.

"So sorry, Mistress, I've missed the bus."

"Sorry, I missed it."

"I've missed the bus Mistress, can we rebook?"

She looked at her phone, not making sense of it at first. As the situation dawned on her, she first smiled at the lucky surprise the stranger on the bus just had but then felt sad and suddenly empty at the thought that he had gotten away when she was sure she would really like to play with him some more.

She toyed with thoughts of an ad in the paper or signs at local bus stops but by the time she got home she had given up those ideas and chalked it up to experience. She felt surprisingly sad about it but resigned to the fact that she had lost him.

She took off her jacket and threw it on the bed, then she started the shower and began to undress. She was down to her stockings and the hot red shoes when she ran her fingers down her side where she had felt his hand steady her. She felt a tingle all the way up her legs. She did it again and felt the tingle again. This time it went from her toes to her waist in the place she had felt him touch her and a tiny, flickering light of hope lit up in her head.

She raced to the bed and grabbed the jacket, fumbling eagerly in the pockets. At first, there was nothing and she almost gave up, but the tingle persisted so she continued and finally she found it. It was there. A business card in her jacket pocket. She read it over several times to make sure it was real. *A barrister*, she thought, and local too. She held the card between her fingers and tapped it on her lips as she was hatching her plan.

First, she would send him the knickers with an anonymous thank you note then wait a couple of days and show up at his office.

This was going to be a lot of fun.

*****

Three Times the Bridesmaid

"When you asked me to be bridesmaid, you never mentioned dressing me like an overripe tomato, or I might have thought twice," I said, only half joking.

"The other bridesmaids aren't complaining," Lisa replied, pointing to her two young cousins doing cartwheels and handstands across the shop in front of the mirrored wall.

"The other bridesmaids are not real humans," I scoffed "They are pieces of elastic with skin and hair! They don't even have bumpy bits to deal with yet, let alone massive excess boobage to tuck into their frocks!"

"There is nothing excess about your boobage. It's fabulous boobage. Tell her, Mum." Lisa poked her mother to get her in on the conversation.

"Lisa is right. Your boobs are your boobs like 'em or not, so you may as well like 'em," Martha chuckled. "And your job as bridesmaid, as far as I can tell, is to be supportive, help the bride into her dress, escort her down the aisle, and look as god awful as possible to make her look good."

Martha chuckled again, this time breaking into a coughing fit, quite amused by her own joke. Once she caught her breath, she continued, "When it is her turn to be your bridesmaid, might I recommend a nice sickly green that will make her look like an overcooked string bean?"

"I'll keep that in mind if I ever find somebody to marry me," I said.

"You're always fishing in the wrong pond, girl, that's your trouble," Martha pointed at me. "You need to stop looking for *Mister Perfect* and then sucking your gut in all the time to try and live up to him. You need to look for a young man who likes your curves and revels in your bumpy bits so much that he feeds you chocolate every day!"

"That sort of man sounds like a mythical beast, Martha," I said, and we all laughed.

The snooty saleswoman came back with more things to try on, but Lisa pointed to one white gown and one red dress. "These are what we would like. Do you have matching ones for the younger girls?"

That was one of the things I loved about Lisa. She wasn't rude, but she was a 'take charge' kind of girl and didn't take shit from anybody. She'd been like that since we met on the first day of school.

The saleswoman looked across at the aspiring gymnasts with such venomous disdain I was afraid they would turn to stone on the spot if they turned around and accidentally made eye contact. She clapped her hands together loudly as if to summon the devil and pointed the young assistant that came running, in the direction of the children.

"Measure them up for size and see what we have for them while I take the adults to try on foundation garments."

Martha put her hands up. "I'll stay here and mind the squad." She gestured towards the kids with her head. "My foundations are beyond help anyway."

Lisa and I giggled as we were led away by the disapproving saleswoman from hell.

It felt like it took an eternity to find the right scaffolding for my generous figure, but once I was all strapped down, laced up and buckled in so that no part of me would dare even think of wobbling, I had to admit I didn't look too bad. Once I put on the dress, I felt pretty good about the whole idea.

Lisa came in and said, "Look at you girl, you look amazing. Here, put these on so they can get the right length for the hem." She handed me the sexiest looking pair of red high heeled shoes I had ever seen.

"Where did these come from?" I asked in disbelief

"A gift from a client at the salon. She heard me saying I wanted red bridesmaids, next thing I knew she had dropped them off with a note wishing me well and when I checked them, they were your size. Put them on, honey, and let me see."

As soon as I put them on, I felt like a million bucks. They were a perfect fit and looked amazing. Even the snooty saleswoman almost cracked out a slight nod of approval.

"Do a spin for me," Lisa encouraged with an appropriate hand gesture.

I walked up and down and did a little turn.

"You are hot stuff, honey. Make sure Gary doesn't see you looking like that too soon, or he might leave me at the altar," she said with a laugh. Then she hugged me. "I am so glad you're my friend, I'd hate to have to hate you."

I couldn't help looking at myself in the mirror as the saleswoman pushed and poked and pinned me to within an inch of my life. I was sure she lingered and adjusted my bust a bit more than was necessary, but I felt so good I didn't really care. As long as she didn't pin me directly, I was happy.

Lisa got the saleswoman to bag up the stuff we were taking with us and told her we'd be back on Thursday for the rest. The saleswoman looked unimpressed, but Lisa didn't seem to notice; she never did. She just expected people to do as she asked, and they usually complied.

The big day came, and everything went off without a hitch. Martha kept everything running to plan by threatening to tell Lisa if anybody even looked like running late. When we got out of the limo at the church, Lisa looked like an angel. Her hair was perfect, her makeup was flawless, and her dress looked like something a Disney princess would envy. I was so proud to be her friend. In fact, the whole bridal party looked fantastic, if I do say so myself.

Gary and his best man Craig looked very handsome in their midnight blue tuxedos, and the four kids looked perfect in their little people's version of the grown-up outfits, and as we did the slow walk down the aisle, I could almost feel people's eyes on me. I felt so amazingly sexy and beautiful I could almost think they were checking me out, but I knew they must have just been eyeing off those amazing shoes.

The reception was mercifully short on speeches and long on good food and drink, but Lisa and I were so scared we would spill on our clothes we didn't really have as much as we would have liked.

When it got to the part of the night where I had to dance with Craig, I was surprised at how good I felt. It was something I had been dreading. At the rehearsal we had been so awkward and stiff together, the idea of all the guests watching that performance made me feel sick.

But when the moment came, I felt like I looked good and Craig seemed less nervous, so we ended up moving well together.

After everybody else had joined us on the floor, we got a bit crowded. At one point, Craig pulled me closer to him to avoid hitting somebody, and I was sure I could feel an erection in his trousers. I suddenly remembered Lisa talking about the trouble he had keeping girlfriends because he was painfully shy and sweet but had an enormous dick and he was rumoured to be a bit of an animal in bed. Apparently, that was a bad combination because he only attracted girls that couldn't handle his size or his enthusiasm. I'd always thought it was a boy-myth until I was sure I felt his length momentarily pressed up against me and I noticed he was blushing but also had a cheeky glint in his eye.

I found myself wishing I could find a man like Craig. A man that was kind, smart and shy but rough enough in bed to keep me happy. I blushed at the thought and the feel of his erection on me and felt a warmth rush from my feet to my belly, but the moment passed very quickly, and we finished the dance without incident. Craig kept us on the dance floor until the end of the next song, and then Lisa broke in. "Let's go get changed so we can eat and drink and party" she practically yelled in my ear to be heard over the music.

Lisa had rooms booked upstairs for the night, so we wouldn't have far to fall after the party. She and Gary would head off on their honeymoon trip in the morning, and I would take her dress back to Martha's place on my way home. So, we headed upstairs to change.

Getting Lisa out of her dress was practically a four-man job but we went carefully, and she helped as much as she could from the inside. Soon she was standing in front of the mirrored wardrobe in nothing but her shoes, stockings, knickers, and a stunning beaded lace corset, all in pristine white. She looked beautiful and I tried not to stare.

"Sexy enough, you think?" she said with a cheeky smile.

"Sure," I replied, in an off-hand sort of way "If you like that sort of thing" I smiled. It was a running joke between us, only I wasn't always sure we were joking. At least I wasn't always sure that I was joking. "Has Gary seen it yet?" I asked in an effort to move past what I feared might turn into an awkward moment.

"Not yet," Lisa chuckled, "But make sure I remember to pack it. I think we shall be playing lots of dress-ups on the honeymoon, so Gary can fill me with babies" Lisa winked at me "I'm hoping for twins, so I can get it over with in one go." She chuckled and showed me her crossed fingers, and the awkward moment had been avoided.

"Now let's get you out of that dress," Lisa said to me.

Mine was not as lavish and only took us a couple of minutes before I was standing next to Lisa in my red satin corset, red knickers, sheer red stockings, and those amazing red shoes. Lisa was standing behind me. I caught a glimpse of our reflection in the mirror and felt a renewed warmth rising from my feet and growing in my belly.

Lisa looked at me in the mirror, taking a long time to examine me from head to toe.

"Damn you look good tonight," she said. "And you're rocking those shoes."

I blushed, and Lisa smiled at me knowingly. "We both look hot, don't we?" she whispered in my ear.

Her words and the sensation of warm breath on my skin made me shudder, the heat in my belly expanding. I tried to speak but couldn't manage to form words, so I nodded just a little.

"To be honest honey, you look hotter than I have ever seen you," Lisa almost purred in a low deep voice as she ran the tip of her finger from my ear to my shoulder, across my bare skin, then gently kissed my neck.

I closed my eyes and wondered if perhaps we had more to drink than I thought, but I heard Lisa's voice gently say "Open your pretty eyes, honey, everything is going to be okay. I promise."

I opened my eyes and looked at Lisa's reflection. Her gaze pinned me, and I could see a glint in her eye as she reached her arms around me and rested her hands on the red satin encasing my bounteous breasts.

"You know all those times when we got drunk and I tried to cop a *friendly* feel?"

I didn't speak, I couldn't, I was trapped in her gaze and stunned by what she was doing, but she continued anyway. "and the times you pretended to be asleep when I touched you through your pyjama top?"

I swallowed hard. We had never spoken about that; it only happened a couple of times and always left me wet and wanting more, but I could never think of a way of encouraging her without the risk of harming our friendship.

"I know you always wanted me to go further, honey," Lisa said, firmly squeezing my breasts. "Tonight, with you looking so hot, I am going to go *much* further if you'll let me."

My thoughts were spinning out of control. It was as if Lisa was reading my mind, or as if we were under some sort of spell, but I didn't need an explanation. I just needed it not to stop. I found the courage to nod, almost imperceptibly.

She let go of my gaze and bent to kiss my neck, gently at first, so softly I barely felt her lips graze my skin, but I saw it in the mirror. Then again, stronger, and I felt the warmth of her mouth. Again, and this time I felt her run the tip of her tongue across my skin. She still had her hands on my breasts squeezing and kneading them through the fabric of the corset and I could feel myself getting wet as I silently prayed to whichever deity could hear me for Lisa to keep going

I'd always been too frightened before but this time I knew. Somehow, I knew in my heart that we would be okay, our friendship would survive; we could do this, and it would all be okay.

She put her hands on my shoulders and whispered warmly in my ear, "Turn around for me honey." I turned, now face to face with my best friend, and I knew we were about to cross a line we had never dared cross before. "Relax girl," Lisa said. "Consider it my wedding gift from you."

She looked into my eyes as if looking for permission. I nodded, so she smiled beautifully before kissing me. The touch of her lips was so soft I might have dreamt it. I could feel a tingle starting in my toes and gradually working its way up my legs as Lisa pressed a little harder and the tip of her tongue ran across my lips gently, softly, tenderly. Then harder and more insistent.

I yielded willingly and soon she was pressing into my mouth and kissing me with a passion I had not felt before. Her tongue was pressed deep, probing and exploring and encouraging mine to do the same. I couldn't help but respond. I had wanted this for so long.

The tingle in my legs was turning into a warm rush and I felt myself getting wetter by the moment. Lisa moved from kissing my mouth to my face and then inched her way down my throat, leaving a warm trail of kisses as she went. She licked and kissed and nibbled at the soft flesh protruding above my corset all the while kneading and squeezing me through the fabric.

I could feel my knickers were soaking wet and I had a deep ache building between my legs. But I was frozen with fear and anticipation. I desperately wanted it, but I was still afraid Lisa would stop and pretend she was joking.

Lisa wrapped her arms around me without taking her lips off my skin. She undid the top of my corset and loosened it enough for her to wrestle one entire breast free from its bonds. She lct out a gasp of delight when she saw it spilling out in all its bounteous glory over the top of the red satin. She grabbed it with both hands and kneaded while she licked and sucked at my nipple until she had it rock hard. I could feel my wetness running down my thigh and I prayed she wouldn't stop.

Lisa sucked my nipple deep into her mouth and I moaned as she flicked it with the hard tip of her tongue. I felt her smile; she knew what she was doing to me, and she seemed to like it. She sucked me harder still and fumbled to release my other breast from the red satin corset.

I was in heaven as she moved her attentions to my newly exposed nipple and began to rub her thumb roughly over the one that was still wet from her warm mouth. I had told her once how much I liked it when a guy did that to me and I wasn't sure if she had remembered or if it was just a fortunate coincidence. Either way, I didn't care. My whole body seemed to be vibrating from my feet up and I was more turned on that I ever thought possible.

Lisa was sucking and biting on one nipple while pinching the other and I could feel the sensations flooding down my body and deep into my groin. She pressed my breasts hard together so that she could bite on both my nipples at once and suddenly I was so awash with sensation that it felt like she was biting directly on my clitoris and I knew she was about to make me orgasm.

I could feel the heat building in my feet and spreading up my legs into my groin and my belly. It exploded in a climax so strong it hit me like a freight train, making my knees tremble and all but buckle. Somehow, I managed to stay on my feet until Lisa said, "Best we get you on the bed honey. Don't want you falling off those shoes."

She guided me gently backwards by the shoulders until I felt the back of my legs make contact with the bed, then she pushed and I fell back, limbs akimbo. Lisa was on top of me in no time, kissing my mouth, biting my lips, and pinching both my nipples between her fingers. It was rough, and it was frenzied, and I loved it.

She pulled and clawed at my corset to give her access to more flesh. She bit me and sucked on me until I was sure I had died and gone to some sort of sexy heaven.

I looked down at Lisa's face. She was glowing. She winked at me, "Might as well be hung for a sheep as a lamb." She slithered to her knees on the floor and lifted my feet in those hot red shoes up onto the bed, then she pushed my knees apart and I suddenly realised what she had in mind. She raised one eyebrow a little as if to check I was okay. I nodded a little more vigorously than I intended, and Lisa laughed. It sounded fabulous.

Lisa began kissing her way from my stockinged knee to the soft flesh of my thigh, softly moaning all the way. When she got to my soaking wet knickers, I was momentarily self-conscious about how wet I was, but Lisa looked up at me. "I don't know what is hotter, honey. These fucking sexy as hell shoes or your soaking wet knickers."

Lisa pulled the slippery wet fabric to one side, exposing me totally and I felt a rush of extra wetness at the thought of it. She grinned an evil lascivious grin and dipped her finger gently in the moisture before bringing it to her lips. She licked it clean and smiled. "Delicious," she said.

Lisa pushed my thighs further apart and kissed my outer lips and ran the tip of her tongue the full length of my pussy. She did it again, pressing her tongue in deeper, and kept repeating the action until she had her tongue pressed deep into me and was ending each stroke with a mind-bending tongue massage of my clitoris. Then she began to eat me in ways I can't even describe. All I knew was that it felt amazing and I found myself wishing I could find a man that could eat pussy like that.

She was licking and nibbling and teasing and kissing, and it all felt like she was enjoying what she was doing to me.

I'd never experienced that before. All the guys I'd been with had spent as little time down there as possible, but Lisa was moaning and eagerly licking and sucking and pressing her whole face into me. I could tell I was going to explode.

I could feel my legs trembling and a searing hot lust beginning in my toes was working its way up my legs, when I noticed Lisa's attention shift for a moment. I looked in the direction I thought had distracted her and saw Gary standing in the doorway watching us.

A massive wave of panic almost overtook me, but Lisa didn't stop what she was doing. Actually, Gary being there seemed to just encourage her. She beckoned him to come closer, pushed my knees further apart, pulled my underwear harder to the side, and pressed her tongue deep into my throbbing wet pussy. I felt my panic give way to the lust that was now possessing me.

The tremble in my legs had moved to encompass my body and I could hear myself moaning and whimpering. I would have begged if I could have formed words. Instead, I made pleading sounds and prayed Lisa would understand. I felt lost in the sensations that were washing over me. The feeling of Lisa's tongue, her lips and her face, the pressure of her hands holding my legs wide apart to ensure Gary could see everything she was doing.

I felt the orgasm start directly under Lisa's tongue and spread like wildfire. Soon I was a throbbing mess as wave after scorching wave of pleasure tore through me relentlessly.

It seemed like it would never end. I shuddered and practically wept. Lisa did not let up at all until I was totally spent, lying back on the bed feeling better than I had ever felt before.

I was only vaguely aware of what was going on around me. I had my eyes closed, but I could feel Lisa was still softly kissing my pussy lips and licking my juices from my thighs. She trailed her fingertips around my wet lips and it felt perfect.

Gary's voice caught my attention, but I wasn't sure who he was talking to. It sounded like one side of a telephone conversation.

"Yeah mate, listen, find Martha and tell her Elvis has left the building and she is in charge for the duration…Yeah, whatever she likes…Yeah, for sure mate then get your arse up to the room as quick as you can…Yep. Yes, just tell her we've started the honeymoon early and hurry. I reckon I'm going to need some help up here bro."

Then all I was aware of was the sound of Lisa's kisses and her warm breath on my skin. I was sure I was being lulled to sleep but when Lisa moved away a little, I was brought back to myself. I opened my eyes and saw her beckon Gary to kiss her.

He grinned a wicked grin and began kissing and licking the juices off her mouth. My juices. He was sucking my wetness from his new bride's mouth and the thought of it sent a warm rush through me, making me moan. Lisa turned and grinned at me.

"Look, baby," she said to Gary. "I think she is ready for some more. Wanna help me? Let's get her knickers off."

Before I even had time to panic, they had slid my knickers down my legs and off. Gary then dropped to his knees next to Lisa and they both began hungrily kissing and licking my thighs, working their way towards my newly aching pussy.

I could feel fingers and tongues and lips, but I couldn't tell who was doing what to me. It was wonderful, and I could feel my juices almost running out of me. Lisa and Gary got into sync and began licking either side of my clit in unison. My aching, throbbing bud was trapped between two seemingly expert tongues and I knew I was about to climax again. I felt the orgasm wash over me, but neither Gary nor Lisa backed off and mere seconds later I felt it again and again.

I lost track of how much they were making me come and I was powerless to do anything but lie there, whimpering and trembling helplessly.

I felt another presence in the room and then Lisa paused what she was doing and said, "Hey, Craig. Care to join us?"

I heard no reply but felt a surge of pleasure when there was suddenly a warm mouth on the soft flesh of my breasts.

I felt Gary move and a second warm mouth was on me. I looked down and saw both the boys, one on each side of me then I heard Lisa's voice.

"Don't be shy, boys," Lisa said. "Our girl here likes those luscious boobies handled nice and rough."

I wasn't sure who moaned their approval to that, it may even have been me, but each of the men grabbed a breast with both their hands and began squeezing and kneading and tugging at me.

"That's it, boys," Lisa said. "Now suck them and bite them, she likes that."

I was in heaven. The guys started to suck and bite at my nipples, flick them with their fingers and pinch them, all at Lisa's urging. I couldn't tell who was doing what anymore and I didn't care. I just wanted more of it, all of it, as much of it as I could get.

Just when I thought it couldn't get any better, I felt Lisa's fingers playing, teasing, sliding around in my wetness then pressing up inside me, filling me, stretching me making me ache so hard I almost cried out with pleasure.

I felt her pressing deep inside me with one hand and beginning to tease my clit with the other. I moaned involuntarily. Lisa laughed "Come on boys. I think our girl here needs to come hard."

Everything seemed to move up a notch. The boys grabbed and bit and sucked and pulled and tugged at my nipples, and Lisa fingered me deep and strong and worked hard on my clit. I couldn't help myself; I began to buck. It was totally beyond my control. Everything was beyond my control. I was being fingered and pleasured and roughly mauled by my best friend and two guys, and I loved it.

My body was no longer my own, it was a plaything for Lisa and whoever else she wanted to share it with. I was lost. Completely lost in the sensation, the lust, the ecstasy and I no longer cared about anything but the pleasure of it. I existed only for that moment, for the feel of mouths and tongues and hands. Only for the sensation, the sounds of sex and the smell of sweat, the arousal and the climaxing. That was all I was for, all I wanted, all I needed, all I could think of.

I became aware of a sensation I wasn't sure I recognised. A warm tingling, throbbing sensation. It started in my toes and moved up until it was encompassing my whole being. It seemed to intensify everything else I could feel to the point of almost unbearable pleasure. I could still feel myself bucking, and I knew I was moaning and whimpering. I realised that the boys and Lisa were practically pinning me down. I began to tremble uncontrollably, and I could hear myself begging, pleading, practically praying but I had no idea what for, what I wanted, where I was going.

The sensations overtook me, and I could sense it coming, the mother of all orgasms was about to overtake me. The heat under Lisa's fingers felt intense and suddenly as if a spark hit fuel, I exploded.

I heard myself cry out and felt my body convulse as I was taken, thrown completely out of myself, set free to float in a warm sea of pure pleasure as if nothing else existed.

At some point, I became aware of three other bodies with me on the bed, all panting. All resting their heads on me as if they had been caught up in my whirlwind and suddenly dropped back to earth.

I looked down at Lisa. She smiled at me beautifully, kissed my thigh and winked before she climbed up higher on the bed and pulled her new husband to her. They became entwined beside me, and I realised I was about to be witness to the consummation of their brand-new marriage.

Despite everything that had just taken place I felt a momentary discomfort at that idea and looked away. I looked down at Craig who also seemed slightly uncomfortable. When we made eye contact, I saw his usual shyness emerge just as he dropped his gaze.

I was tempted to try to sneak away and let the happy couple go at it, but when I went to move, I noticed Craig was staring down at my shoes. I felt compelled to hold still and let him look. He stared at them for ages then I watched his eyes as they traced up my legs and along my body, resting for a long time on my breasts which still spilt out over the top of my disarrayed corset. The breasts which, although I couldn't see them clearly from that angle, I knew must be bruised and marked from the recent activity.

Part of me thought I should feel self-conscious, but I didn't. I was enjoying his gaze. It made me feel warm and beautiful... or maybe that was the shoes. Either way, I laid still and let him look. Craig finally looked up and made eye contact with me. He smiled and brushed the hair off my face; my heart almost melted.

He motioned towards my breasts and said, almost coyly, "I hope we weren't too rough."

"No," I replied without thinking. "Not at all. I quite like it like that. Couldn't you tell?" Then I felt suddenly shy and looked down.

Craig put two fingers under my chin and lifted my face back up to look into my eyes.

"Yes," he said. "I could tell," He smiled again with just a hint of cheekiness in his eyes.

I'm sure I blushed. I felt all a quiver, like a silly school girl who had just been noticed by her crush.

He ran the back of his fingers gently down my cheek then cupped my face in his hand and simply looked at me. Looked at me with a serious expression as if some internal dialogue was going on.

Then he smiled again, and asked softly, "May I kiss you?"

"Yes," I replied, like some coy maiden. "I'd like that."

Lisa and Gary were getting pretty hot and heavy on the bed right next to me, but the moment Craig's lips touched mine I lost all awareness of them.

He kissed me so softly, so tenderly I almost cried. Then he pulled away and looked at me again.

"We danced well together tonight," he said in a serious tone. "And you looked so good in that dress and those amazing shoes." He paused and swallowed then continued, "I was hoping to have the courage to ask you out before we got…. um… side-tracked." he said with an almost apologetic grin.

Part of me was so dumbfounded I was speechless, but another part of me was feeling more courageous and piped up. "How about you kiss me some more, and we talk about that later?"

"Very good plan," he said with a tiny chuckle and then he kissed me again, only this time with more urgency and more passion.

His mouth tasted sweet and warm and good as our tongues swirled around together, exploring each other, learning each other. I could feel myself getting wet all over again and I loved it.

Craig kissed my cheek, my mouth, my eyes then looked at me. He motioned to Gary and Lisa just beside us going at it like rabbits. "Shall we?"

"I think so," I said with a wink.

Craig moved down to my breasts and was extremely gentle, kissing and licking them and sucking them into his mouth, but the heat was building, and soon he was biting one nipple and pinching the other, and I was squirming under his touch.

"God, you're beautiful" he practically growled at me "I need to taste you."

"Yes," I responded eagerly. "Anything, please take anything you want."

He looked at me with a wide grin and before I knew it, he had spread me wide apart and was plunging his tongue deep into my aching pussy. I'd never had a tongue go so deep inside me before. It felt so good. He licked and probed and lapped at my juices as he held my thighs tight in his hands. I'd never noticed how big his hands were before, but they felt so good gripping tight around my legs, holding them apart for his attention.

When he sucked my clit into his mouth and flicked it back and forth with his tongue, I climaxed over and over until I found myself fighting him and trying to pull away, but he held me firm and didn't relent. I didn't really want him to stop but struggling against him felt incredible.

Finally, Craig released me from his mouth. He moved off the bed and stood on the floor. He had such a strong, determined look on his face that I felt totally safe - controlled and safe. He undressed, and I watched, spellbound by the amazing body being unveiled before me. I was sure I'd seen him with his shirt off before, but I'd never noticed just how fit and hot he was. When he dropped his boxers, I almost gasped at the size of his hard-on. He winked at me, grabbed my ankles and pulled me to the edge of the bed.

Still holding my ankles, he admired my shoes then kissed each of them before he pushed my legs back and up exposing me completely. It made me shudder with a pleasant sense of humiliation. Then he growled in a low, dominating tone, "I'm going to fuck you, unless you object."

I shuddered again but managed to nod.

"Good girl," he said in a way that made my juices flow and my pussy ache.

He rubbed his enormous erection along the length of my dripping wet pussy until he was slick with my juices.

"Guide me into you, beautiful," he urged in a deliciously commanding tone.

I reached down and felt his gorgeous cock, hard in my hand, and was suddenly hungry for it. I pressed the head of his stunning erection against myself and held him there as he pushed, strong but slow. I felt myself stretch around his head and I momentarily felt nervous.

"Relax, angel," he reassured me. "You can do this."

His voice, his tone, everything about him made me believe that, and I relaxed. As I did I could feel Craig push into me further and it felt so good. I smiled up at him. He held my gaze as he kept working himself into me, little by little.

"You can let go now," he said with a grin. "I'm not going to fall out."

I let go and put my hand back beside me. It found Lisa's hand. I had almost forgotten she and Gary were there. She grabbed my hand and held it. I liked that. It felt right.

Craig still held my gaze as he began to slide himself slowly in and out of me. I was so wet and so turned on now that he was inside me that he moved easily.

The way he looked into my eyes as he began to truly fuck me, made my knees turn to jelly. I could feel from the way Lisa squeezed my hand that she was having a great time with whatever Gary was doing to her, but I was mesmerised by the eyes of the man who was inside of me, stretching me, filling me and making me feel whole.

I could see tiny beads of sweat forming on his brow as if he was straining. I realised he was straining to contain himself. I wanted him to let go, to take me like a beast. I knew I could handle it. I wanted it.

I stared into his eyes and tried to form words. It wasn't easy, but I managed, finally, to say, "Take me like you want to, Craig."

He grinned at me. He let go of my ankles, pressed his weight down on my body and whispered into my ear. "Wrap those legs around me like a hot little bitch and let me fuck your brains out, beautiful." That just made me moan and I heard him all but chuckle in my ear.

I wrapped my legs around him, so the red shoes were resting on his back. I felt his breath on my neck just before he bit down hard on me and made me scream. It felt so good, a renewed flood of wetness surrounded his cock and I felt him smile against my skin.

He drove his cock into me hard, again and again. I could feel I was taking him completely, all of him, deep into me with every thrust.

He pounded into me like the beast I wanted him to be, fucking me, biting me, grabbing at my tits, squeezing them and shaking them by the nipples. I was in heaven. I could hear grunting and groaning, and I had no idea which of the four of us it was. I knew Gary was fucking Lisa beside me and she was still holding my hand.

I heard pleading and moaning and begging and intermittent cries of close to anguished pleasure. I knew I was whimpering, and I could feel Craig grunting. The look on his face was pure ecstasy and I reached up to pull his face to mine and kiss him.

His kiss was amazing, hot, strong, powerful and I wanted it to last forever. He sucked my tongue into his mouth and bit it almost too hard, then he bit my lips and forced his tongue into my mouth, as I felt another orgasm wash over me. He groaned into my ear as he felt my pussy walls contract around him and growled, "Good girl." Then he upped his speed and began to fuck me harder and faster than I would have thought possible.

I felt myself being lost in the pleasure again until I heard Craig's voice in my ear. "Touch your clit and come for me one more time, beautiful. Then I want to fuck your tits."

Just hearing him say that was nearly enough to push me over the edge but I dutifully pushed my hand down between us and massaged my clit until I exploded again. He knew. Craig could tell when I orgasmed. I'd never had a guy who knew or even cared before.

"Good girl. My beautiful, good girl," he said and smiled at me.

He slid himself out of me and I couldn't help feeling sad, but he kissed my nose and said, "It won't be the last time Angel, I promise you that"

Then he moved himself up and pressed his cock between my breasts, squeezing them hard around him. When he began to fuck my tits, I realised that I could easily reach him with my mouth on each thrust.

He thrust, and I sucked the head of his gorgeous cock until I could tell he was about to come. I pushed his butt to show I wanted him in my mouth and within seconds I was rewarded with the best sound I could imagine; the sound of a hot man calling my name as he was coming in my mouth.

Up until that point I wasn't even sure he knew it but each time he said my name, it was like a bell went off in my brain, and I knew I was never letting this one get away. Never. He was perfect.

When he finished, he moved to kiss me and wrap me in his arms. He kissed my forehead. Lisa let go of my hand and hugged into my back, kissing my neck and shoulder gently. I felt Gary put his arm around his new wife. I felt my shoes fall off and I kicked them onto the floor. I snuggled in between my best friend and the man I knew, in that moment, I was going to marry and fell into the best sleep I had ever had.

I did end up choosing green for the bridesmaid's dress, and Lisa looked beautiful in it. Although she looked more like a pea pod than a bean, but what do you expect with two babies on board?

*****

A Christmas Carol

Jennifer hadn't been at Carol & Carol very long and could think of an array of things she would rather be doing than going to an office Christmas party full of people she didn't know well and didn't much like. But Sharon, her flatmate and work colleague, had insisted it was the best way to connect with people and advance up the company ladder - and advancing up the ladder was exactly what Jennifer intended to do.

She had a plan. She had moved away from all the things that she felt were holding her back and she planned to be wealthy before she was thirty. She had no desire to be 'Jenny from accounts' any longer than she had to be. She was determined to be going places, sooner rather than later.

With that in mind, she had dressed to the nines and was sitting in the back of a taxi with Sharon, on their way to the office on an otherwise normal Saturday night.

She hadn't brought many clothes with her in the move and hadn't purchased anything new yet, other than some work outfits, so she was limited in her choices. She had gone with a mid-thigh length black and red checked skirt that hugged her hips and bottom very flatteringly and black lace stockings that clung snugly to her thighs. They had a line of tiny red roses up the back, which took some effort to get straight, but were worth it.

She topped the outfit off with an elegant white blouse and a thin length of red velvet ribbon tied in an elaborate bow at her neck. She was originally wearing black shoes but as she was leaving home, her newly-wed neighbour spotted her and gave her a stunning pair of red high heels. They were a perfect fit, suited the outfit beautifully, and made Jennifer feel sexier than she had since the breakup.

The taxi driver kept sneaking looks at her in the rear-view mirror. She was tempted to tell him to keep his eyes on the road, but she could hear her former fiancés words ringing in her ears, and it made her keep quiet. For the moment anyway.

"You're a stuck up, cold-hearted bitch, Jennifer, and nobody likes you," he had said, as some sort of excuse for sleeping with her sister just weeks before the wedding.

His words had stung... Really stung, almost as much as his actions, and left Jennifer speechless at the time for fear of letting him see her cry.

But now, sitting in a taxi thousands of miles away and on her way to a party at her new job with her new flatmate starting her new life, she wished they could both see her. She wished her ex and her sister could hear her. She wished she could tell them her plans. She was going places.

She was going to succeed. She was going to travel, be wealthy and successful, and one way or another she was going to make sure she never had to rely on a man again.

She looked down at herself and smiled. She felt good, attractive, sexy even. Those shoes really suited her outfit, and she was suddenly sure she was going to have a good night.

When they arrived, the party was already in full swing. Sharon ushered Jennifer to the bar and ordered two glasses of champagne. Sharon had assured Jennifer she would introduce her to all the important people. Instead, she downed her drink as if it was water and quickly disappeared into a sea of men who seemed to be cheering and chanting her name. When Jennifer looked at the faces, they were all men she knew from the accounts department. She couldn't see anything to be gained there, so she didn't bother to follow.

Jennifer looked around the room, trying to get a feel for the people. Trying to see if she could pick who she should talk to, but everybody seemed to be busy chatting and drinking in their private groups. She decided to stand back and watch, at least for a while. She toyed with the idea of leaving, but her inner voice said she would make no progress if she baulked at the first hurdle. So, she stood and waited for a possible opening to start up a conversation with somebody.

She might have felt self-conscious standing on her own at a party on another night, but she felt quite relaxed and comfortable tonight. Maybe it was the champagne, maybe it was that nobody seemed to notice her, or maybe it was those killer sexy red shoes.

Whatever it was, she was happy to stand and people watch, waiting for the right opportunity to present itself.

She had no idea how long she just stood there. Everybody seemed to be so involved in their conversations it was like Jennifer was invisible. She liked that. Now and then she would look over to where the rest of the accounts team were. It seemed as if Sharon was involved in a drinking game with a bunch of guys that looked like they were groping her at every opportunity and Sharon was squirming and giggling.

If they were better friends, Jennifer thought, or if they had known each other longer she might go and rescue Sharon from herself. They weren't though, and Jennifer had the distinct impression that Sharon would not appreciate the interference.

Jennifer suddenly felt like she was being watched. She turned casually around but couldn't see anybody that wasn't deeply engaged in a conversation. Shrugging it off, she went back to her people watching. She found herself wondering if she could gauge the importance of a person by the body language of the people around them. She couldn't.

Then Jennifer felt it again, the sensation of somebody's eyes on her. She tried to ignore it but eventually she couldn't help scanning the room to see who it was, but still could not see a likely candidate.

While Jennifer was looking around the room she noticed one of the big bosses, Miss Carol, standing at the bar on her own, as if waiting for something. Jennifer wondered if that was who had been looking at her, even though she was looking away at that moment.

The company was owned and run by two siblings and it was widely rumoured that the sister, Miss Carol, was the true power. Jennifer took the opportunity to have a good look at the woman who was reputed to run the company with an iron fist. Jennifer had seen her before, at the panel interview she had for the job, and had also seen her around the building from time to time but had never been able to truly look at her until now.

She was an older woman, perhaps mid to late fifties. Steel grey hair pulled back into a severe bun, as usual. She was wearing almost all black. A knee length pencil skirt and matching jacket, black medium-high heels with a dark blue blouse. Not much different from what she would wear around the office. She looked stylish, stern, and intimidating as always.

From the other side of the room, Sharon squealed loudly and then burst into a fit of laughter. Jennifer looked and saw two of the guys now had their hands up Sharon's top. Jennifer looked away feeling a mixture of pity and disgust.

She turned back to finish checking out Miss Carol only to find she was gone. Jennifer was momentarily disappointed.

"Very nice shoes." The voice behind Jennifer caught her by surprise. She turned around to see Miss Carol standing just behind her, holding a bottle of champagne.

Jennifer tried not to look startled and worked to gather her thoughts as quickly as she could but before she could respond Miss Carol spoke again.

"Are you not joining your friend?"

Jennifer took a deep breath and tried to sound in control of her voice.

"No, I don't think it is my sort of party over there."

"I didn't think so," Miss Carol replied with a tone that Jennifer couldn't quite pick. "If you are only going to watch the proceedings, you could always join me in my office. I'm heading back up there now if you would care to accompany me."

She pointed to what looked like large glass windows above the conference room they were standing in and continued, "The view is better and without so much noise."

Jennifer was dumbstruck and couldn't move. This was probably the exact chance she was hoping for, but she was paralysed by it. As if they had a mind of their own, her feet took two steps in the direction Miss Carol was indicating and then two more and soon Jennifer was following probably the most powerful person in the company up to her office.

As they reached the bottom of the stairs, Miss Carol paused and gestured for Jennifer to go first. "It's the big door at the top. You can't miss it."

Jennifer was sure she could feel the older woman's eyes on her all the way up the stairs but decided she must be admiring the shoes. They were very eye-catching.

The large door opened into an empty office and Jennifer thought she had made a mistake. But Miss Carol moved to a second, inner door and said, "Here we are"

The second office was stunning. There was an enormous, ornately carved desk, with matching chairs, a large leather reclining chair with a reading lamp and an enormous bookshelf. The external windows looked out over the harbour which looked beautiful in the moonlight. But it was the internal view that amazed Jennifer. The walls were one-way glass from floor to ceiling. It made her wonder if the people downstairs would behave differently if they knew they were so easily watched.

She got her bearings and spotted her own desk, clearly visible in the background. The whole situation felt a little surreal. She had only come along to the party in the hope of making some connections with somebody higher up. Now she was almost frightened of how

high she seemed to be going but she took a breath and decided to go with it, with whatever happened.

Jennifer could see Sharon, now very drunk, being groped and fondled by numerous guys.

Miss Carol stood so close that Jennifer could smell the older woman's perfume. She shuddered as she felt Miss Carol's warm breath on the back of her neck.

"Are you cold Jennifer?" she asked in a comforting voice that was rich and smooth like pipe tobacco. "It is Jennifer isn't it?"

"Yes, Miss Carol - I mean no, Miss Carol - I mean…" Jennifer stammered, realising she was not making the impression she wanted. She looked down at her feet the way she used to when she was in trouble as a child. She hadn't done that for years. She struggled for a moment. Her fear of not making a good impression was robbing her of her usual confidence. She saw the gorgeous red shoes and told herself *snap out of it if you don't want to blow this*.

She looked up, turned enough to make eye contact, took a deep breath and said with as steady a voice as she could, "No, I'm not cold, and yes, it is Jennifer. Thank you, Miss Carol," She then realised that her hair had not all fallen back into place when she lifted her head and she almost dropped it again in embarrassment, but she managed to stand firm.

Miss Carol smiled, raised her hand slowly and brushed the hair from Jennifer's face.

"Good girl. I'd much prefer a wolf to a lamb any day," Miss Carol commented as if she had been privy to Jennifer's thoughts. Those words, the intimate gesture and the deep smokey voice made Jennifer shudder again and sent a wave of tingling warmth from her toes to her scalp.

Her boss just smiled and Jennifer realised that despite her severe style and manner, Miss Carol was quite an attractive woman in a stern and commanding way.

"Would you like another drink, Jennifer?" the older woman asked, as she moved to the desk and poured two glasses.

Jennifer was beginning to enjoy the way her boss was using her name. She hated it being shortened, but people did it anyway. 'Jenny' or 'Jen' always sounded like a name for a child or a pet, but people so often got offended when she insisted on Jennifer.

"Yes, please Miss Carol," Jennifer replied and put her hand out to take the glass offered.

Miss Carol held the glass and Jennifer's gaze for just a heartbeat longer than necessary, sending another tingling rush through the young woman's body.

Jennifer began to feel like she was being played, like a harp in the hands of a skilled musician, and she liked it.

Both women turned to look out over the party again. The older woman began pointing out people and mentioning their names and positions. Something in the tone made the younger woman feel the need to make mental notes to help her remember.

As they scanned the room below they were brought to where Sharon had moved into an empty office. She was in the middle of a huddle and on her knees, quite obviously giving one of her colleagues a head job. The others in the room seemed to be expecting a turn too.

Jennifer felt extremely uncomfortable and tried not to draw any attention to the situation, but her boss said calmly, "Your friend is a very silly girl if she thinks that will get her a decent promotion."

Both women were silent for a moment and just watched the proceedings. Jennifer relaxed a little. Her boss was obviously not thrown or surprised by what Sharon was doing.

"You can't rise higher than the dick you're sucking," both the women said at the same time.

The younger woman blushed at the synchronicity. The older woman simply smiled and nodded. "Indeed. Now, if she had the courage to walk up to my brother's office and offer to suck his dick like that she could really go places."

Jennifer was a bit shocked by the casualness of that remark but not enough to stop her from asking, "Would she really?"

"Yes, of course," the older woman said with a grin "He will be in his office watching that right now. Probably with his trousers around his ankles. She does this every year, so he would have been watching for it. I'm expecting things to heat up quite a bit down there shortly. That will amuse my brother no end. They forget how clearly those cubicle offices can be seen from up here."

"But would she really get a promotion out of it?" Jennifer asked.

"Yes, almost certainly." The reply came with a sly grin. "Why, are you thinking of giving it a try?"

Jennifer suddenly felt very self-conscious and looked at her feet again, "No Miss Carol, not at all."

The older woman put two fingers under Jennifer's chin, lifting her face and fixing her with a gaze that was powerful but obviously not at full intensity. Jennifer decided this would be the wrong woman to cross if she wanted to live to tell the tale.

Miss Carol held Jennifer's head up and examined her face for what seemed like minutes before she said, "Relax Jennifer. I was only teasing. I am hoping your ambitions might lie elsewhere. And there's no need to be quite so formal; when we are alone, you can call me Miss."

Jennifer wanted to hide but couldn't do anything to break her boss's gaze other than blink. Once she did, the older woman moved her fingers from beneath Jennifer's chin, running the tips of them gently down her throat to the red velvet bow at her neck. Jennifer could feel herself blushing. Her heart was beating so hard in her chest she was sure that Miss Carol could practically hear it.

"I love this bow, Jennifer. It matches those gorgeous shoes perfectly," Miss Carol remarked, gently toying with the strand of velvet at Jennifer's neck. "In fact, I quite like your whole outfit, it shows off your...*style* very well." During the pause in speech, Jennifer felt a tremendous rush of heat flood up from her feet to her face. Miss Carol traced her fingertips across

Jennifer's brow and pushed her long dark hair back behind her shoulder.

"You are an exceptionally beautiful girl, Jennifer, and seemingly smart and ambitious. I like those traits in a young woman. But I wonder just how smart and how ambitious you are." The older woman looked into Jennifer's eyes and spoke in a soft low tone. "I wonder if you can see a perfect opportunity when it arises, and if you have the courage to reach out and take it."

Jennifer said nothing at all. She was frozen, trapped in this woman's thrall. Unable to move and not really wanting to.

"I'm willing to bet you have what it takes to take advantage of your current situation, Jennifer," Miss Carol pulled the free end of the velvet bow, causing it to slide undone. Jennifer could now hear her pulse beating loudly in her ears. She had no idea what was about to happen, but she knew she wanted it.

The older woman removed the ribbon completely and dropped it on the desk. She started on the buttons at Jennifer's throat and soon had her blouse undone. She pulled the blouse open enough to expose the tender flesh pressed up just above Jennifer's bra. She smiled a lascivious smile. "Very nice, Jennifer, very nice indeed." She bent forward and kissed the soft bulge gently. "I am about to take you, my sweet girl, and do with your lovely body as I please. I will do you no harm, but I do not like to be interrupted, so if you wish me to stop it is best you say so now. Do you want me to stop, Jennifer?"

The directness of the question and the power of her boss's gaze made it difficult for Jennifer to form a clear thought. But she knew she did not want this to stop, whatever this was, and she knew she didn't want to stumble and stammer and sound unsure, so she gathered all her strength and managed to clearly say, "No Miss, I don't want you to stop."

"Good girl," the older woman said in that tone that Jennifer was growing to love. "I am sure you will not regret your decision, unlike your very slutty friend downstairs." Miss Carol gestured toward the window, but Jennifer didn't look. She didn't care; she was lost in her own destiny and could do nothing to save Sharon from hers.

The older woman grinned as if she knew full well the effect she was having on her young visitor. She moved to kiss Jennifer's neck and pushed the blouse back off her shoulders, down her arms. She kissed along Jennifer's shoulder and pushed the shirt completely off, letting it fall to the floor.

Jennifer's mind was awash with thoughts she couldn't control. She felt embarrassed, self-conscious and deeply aroused, as her boss held her at arm's length drinking in the sight of her young body. Miss Carol nodded her approval then cupped the lace covered breasts in her hands, squeezing and kneading them as she ran the tip of her tongue along the cleavage and kissed and nipped at the soft flesh protruding above the bra.

Jennifer's skin tingled under the warm touch of her boss's mouth and she felt her nipples harden. Miss Carol pressed her palm to Jennifer's chest to feel her heart and said with a broad grin, "My, my young Jennifer your little heart is pounding. Are you afraid my dear, or are you aroused?"

Jennifer struggled to make sense of the question. Her mind was foggy as if under the spell of this powerful older woman. It took her a moment or two, but she managed to say "Both, Miss."

"Good," the older woman said, "Turn around for me."

Jennifer turned her back on Miss Carol and was gently pushed forward towards the desk.

"Bend over for me, Jennifer," she said, "I want to look at what you have under your skirt."

Jennifer bent over and rested her hands on the desk. Her boss lifted the skirt up over Jennifer's hips, revealing her underwear and the tops of her stockings and thighs. Jennifer felt exposed, vulnerable, and more turned on than she thought she should be.

"Lovely," the older woman said, more to herself than anything as she began to rub her hands over Jennifer's bottom and hips, then extended her touch to the bare skin between her stockings and her underwear. The sensation of her boss's hands on her thighs was causing a deep ache between Jennifer's legs and was making it difficult for her to breathe.

"Bend more and spread your legs," the older woman said in a more forceful, dominating tone Jennifer hadn't heard before. It sent a shimmering thrill from her feet to her hot, flushed face. She bent and shuffled her feet further apart, then heard what she wanted to hear: "Good girl."

Jennifer felt her boss's hands kneading and squeezing her flesh and was aching, desperately aching to be touched more intimately. She had no idea what was going to come of this encounter, but she was so turned on she didn't really care. If she ended up getting the sack, she could always find another job. But on some level, she was confident that was not going to happen. She felt sure this was going to serve her well and at least get her out of accounts and on the next rung up the ladder.

She honestly didn't care if she was wrong. She was so hot for Miss Carol right at that moment she would do anything for it to never stop. She felt her boss pull down the back of her underwear, slowly baring her rounded cheeks, and the thrill increased to where Jennifer could barely think straight.

"You have such a beautiful bottom, Jennifer, even more beautiful than it promised to be under that skirt," the older woman said as she ran her fingertips lightly over every inch of the exposed skin. "I do love the look of your underwear pushed down like that, Jennifer, like a naughty child waiting to be spanked, but I think it is time for you to take them off for me,"

Jennifer was so lost in some erotic dream state she took a moment to register what Miss Carol had said.

"Now please, Jennifer" The tone was so commanding that it snapped Jennifer out of her reverie and she scrambled to comply as quickly as she could. She slid her now soaking wet knickers down her legs and stepped out of them.

"Now hand them to me," the command came. Jennifer complied.

"Good girl" came the soothing reward. "Now pass me a glove out of the bottom draw please, Jennifer, then bend back over for me and spread those delicious legs. I am going to see how tight you are."

Jennifer opened the bottom drawer and found a box of black latex gloves. Her mind went into a bit of a spin about why they were there and what they were for, but she pushed down her fear. She wanted this, whatever this was. She handed a glove to Miss Carol and then dutifully bent over and placed her hands on the desk.

She felt a mixture of fear and excitement rising from her feet. She had never been touched by a woman before. She had never even considered it and yet, she suddenly wanted it desperately.

"Lower," the older woman instructed, and Jennifer pressed herself down onto the desk "Good girl. Now really spread those pretty legs for me."

Jennifer shuffled her feet as far apart as the red shoes would allow and realised she had never felt so exposed or vulnerable before in her life. That thought sent a rush of blood to her groin and she felt her wetness spreading down her thighs.

She knew Miss Carol was standing behind her, looking at her body and it increased her sense of vulnerability but also her eagerness to comply.

Jennifer heard the snapping sound of the glove as her boss put it on and it sent a shiver through her. She felt a hand on her naked backside as if Miss Carol were steadying herself then she felt fingers sliding between her wet pussy lips.

"You are so very wet Jennifer," the older woman said. "I like that, it is better for both of us. Better still if you enjoy what I do to you."

Miss Carol teased and explored Jennifer's slippery swollen lips until her hand was nicely wet.

Jennifer inhaled sharply as she felt her boss plunge deep up inside her with no hesitation. It caught her by surprise. There was no pain but tremendous pressure. The older woman paused a moment to let Jennifer catch her breath and then the pressure increased. Jennifer assumed it was fingers inside her, but she couldn't tell for sure. All she could feel was pressure. Deep, thrilling, throbbing pressure and she moaned.

"Do you like that Jennifer?" The question seemed to not require an answer. "You are very tight my dear. Deliciously tight. I like that."

Jennifer could hear the words as if she was overhearing a conversation from another room, but they didn't mean all that much to her. She was lost in the sensation of being filled and stretched. If she had any thought at all, it was how good it felt to be taken like that and used for her boss's pleasure, how much she was aching, how wet she was, and how she had never felt so good before in her life.

Miss Carol pressed deep into Jennifer. Deep and hard. Eliciting a series of gentle low moans from her lips.

She could feel her boss's eyes all over her body. Drinking her in. Admiring every part of her. She felt the burning gaze, like a hot fingertip, following the line of red roses down the backs of her legs to her sexy hot shoes. Then she felt her boss shudder and moan as if hit by a wave of intense, satisfying pleasure.

Miss Carol slowly slid her fingers out of Jennifer, making the young woman moan with disappointment.

"Relax Jennifer, "This doesn't have to end here, unless you want it to, but we need to talk. Stand up and pull yourself together for a few moments."

Jennifer stood up, feeling deliciously dazed and dishevelled. She tried to straighten herself up and make sense of the evening, but with little success. She did manage to pull her skirt down and lean her backside against the desk. She looked up at the older woman who looked back sternly but then reached out a hand to push the hair off Jennifer's face.

"Are you okay, Jennifer?" she asked.

The young woman nodded although she was reluctant to move at all.

"I would prefer it if I knew you could speak, Jennifer. Now please, pull yourself together,"

Her deep, commanding voice cut straight through Jennifer's fog and snapped her out of it.

"Yes Miss, sorry. It's just that you…well…you just…" Jennifer trailed off and just shrugged, feeling unusually helpless and afraid she was disappointing her boss.

But the older woman smiled. "I am well aware of what I was just doing Jennifer." She smirked. "I'm also aware of how you might be feeling but we need to talk before we go any further, I'm afraid. Are you with me enough for that?" she asked

Jennifer straightened herself up and rubbed her hands over her face. She returned the older woman's gaze and said as firmly as she could manage, "Yes, Miss Carol. I am fine to talk."

"Good girl," came the response. "Very good girl."

The older woman encouraged Jennifer to sit up on the desk and stood in front of her.

"Now, Jennifer. Do you enjoy working here?"

Jennifer suddenly felt afraid that she was about to lose her job after all. Her head dropped, and she looked at her shoes, then instantly felt her confidence return. She squared her shoulders, took a deep breath and said, "Yes, Miss Carol. I love working here." Then she had a rush of blood to her brain and added, "But I don't want to be in accounts forever."

The older woman smirked and chuckled a little "No, I didn't think so, Jennifer. I had something else in mind for you. How would you like to be my assistant? The outer office has been vacant for a while, and I'd like it to be yours if you are interested."

Jennifer's jaw dropped open, and it took some effort for her to form a coherent answer. But Miss Carol waited patiently with a casual smirk on her face.

"I would love that, Miss Carol," was the best she could manage.

"Would you like to know what the job entails?" the older woman said with one eyebrow raised in obvious amusement.

"Yes Miss Carol, I would like to know what the job entails," Jennifer said, "I'm sorry, I'm overwhelmed and still feeling a bit scattered."

The older woman smiled and looked almost softly at Jennifer.

"I understand my dear and I am quite pleased that I have managed to scatter and overwhelm you, but you do need to understand what will be expected of you before you accept."

Miss Carol went on to explain in detail what the job would entail but went to great lengths to assure Jennifer that she would not be expected to be up to speed immediately.

"To begin with, Jennifer, we need to get your passport in order; I have a trip coming up that I will want you to accompany me on. Then the most important thing you will be expected to do is keep people out of my office as much as possible. I need a lioness at my door. One that even my brother won't cross. A lioness that will bow to nobody but me." Then she fixed Jennifer with her gaze.

"Do you understand Jennifer?"

"Yes, Miss Carol."

"Good girl. You will start off on the equivalent salary of a section head, and it will rise as you get more experience and take on more responsibility. If you perform well, you could be the highest paid employee here before the next Christmas party. Does that suit you?"

"Yes, Miss. Of course, Miss," Jennifer said not sure what else she could possibly say.

Miss Carol smiled and looked Jennifer up and down "You really are a delight," she smiled. "There is another aspect of the job that you need to understand clearly Jennifer," she said. "A more personal and more demanding aspect."

Jennifer looked into the older woman's eyes and prayed it involved being touched again.

There was a painfully long pause as Miss Carol seemed to be gathering her thoughts.

"I want more than just to seduce you, Jennifer. More than some Christmas party fun. I want to touch you, to teach you, possess you and protect you. In short, I want to own you Jennifer, body and soul." There was another pause and Jennifer was almost afraid to breathe.

"If you accept the position, I will require you to be available to me at all times, Jennifer. Physically available, sexually available. I want to be able to touch you when I wish, where I wish and however I wish. Do you understand what I am saying to you?"

Jennifer's head was buzzing, but she knew she needed to respond.

"Yes, Miss Carol," she said as clearly as she could.

"Are you still interested in the job, Jennifer?"

"Yes, Miss. Very much so, Miss."

"Good girl. Just to be very clear... I will be free to take you if and when I want. No matter where we are or who we are with. You will submit to my wishes without resistance at all times. Is that clear?"

"Yes, Miss," Jennifer said, feeling herself begin to tremble.

"I will generally be discrete here at work, but there are situations where I will expose you to people and let them see what I am doing to you. Will that bother you, Jennifer?"

Jennifer was struggling to breathe, struggling to think straight, struggling to even accept that the situation was real. She was confused, aroused, and having trouble focusing but she knew she wanted this. It was not an idea that had ever occurred to her before, but now that it was on offer she wanted it more than anything else she could think of.

"Will that bother you, Jennifer?" the older woman repeated in a much sterner voice.

Jennifer took one brief moment to draw breath and let her thoughts take form, then fixed her boss with as firm a gaze as she could muster and replied. "No Miss, it won't bother me. I look forward to it. I will happily submit to your wishes, no matter what."

Miss Carol smiled broadly and cupped Jennifer's face in her hand. "You are perfect," she said. "We will have to speak at length about what you will and will not be required to do, but I do not wish to waste much more of our time tonight. So, I'll say briefly that you will not be expected to touch me or gratify me in any way other than being available for my pleasure. There are times when I will hurt you, but I will not harm you. Are you following me, Jennifer?"

"Yes, Miss," the younger woman said, feeling far too turned on to want to keep talking.

"Good girl," came the delicious reply. "As well as your salary I will provide an apartment, a car and driver, and an account for all your food, clothes, and other needs. You will find I am very generous when I am happy Jennifer and I believe you will make me very happy."

Jennifer was shaking almost uncontrollably, whether from fear or excitement or arousal she couldn't tell but she knew she was wet. She could feel it running down her thighs.

"Enough talk for today, Jennifer. Undress for me now; I want to see all of you."

Jennifer undid her bra and let it fall to the floor. Then she unzipped her skirt and let that fall too before stepping out of it. She went to push her stockings down, but Miss Carol said, "Leave them and those gorgeous shoes. I like them."

Miss Carol looked at the near-naked younger woman and smiled appreciatively. She moved close and pressed herself against Jennifer, pinning her to the desk. She ran her hand up Jennifer's back and closed her fist tightly around a handful of hair, pulling her head to the side, then ran a warm tongue up Jennifer's neck to her jaw.

Jennifer could feel hot breath on her skin, and it made her all but melt. She couldn't believe she was here, doing this. Or letting it be done to her, more accurately. She felt so good, so hot, so aroused and she never wanted to come down.

Miss Carol slid her free hand down Jennifer's torso and belly, finding her way to the hot wet mess she had created between Jennifer's legs. She smiled her approval as she began to caress and tease the soft wet lips. Circling and sliding her fingertips between them as she whispered, "You are perfect, Jennifer, I want to consume you entirely." into the younger woman's ear. Then she moved her fingers to Jennifer's clitoris and pinched it hard until the younger woman let out a whimper. Jennifer wasn't sure if she was feeling pleasure or pain, but she didn't care.

"Good girl," the warm voice said in her ear. "I like that."

The hand in Jennifer's hair pulled back sharply and the older woman bit her way down the exposed neck and along one shoulder. All the while pinching and tugging at Jennifer's now blood-filled nub rougher than anyone had ever dared.

Jennifer's head was a whirling mess of pleasure, arousal and anticipation. She couldn't remember ever being so turned on, but at that moment she could barely remember her own name. She was aching and wet and needed to orgasm desperately. Her legs were trembling, and she wasn't sure she could keep standing for much longer. She felt herself being pushed backwards and was powerless to resist.

"Lay back on the desk now, Jennifer," came the instruction.

Jennifer laid back and could feel her boss's eyes all over her.

"Make your nipples hard for me," The older woman commanded.

Jennifer cupped her breasts in her hands and massaged and squeezed them, then strummed her fingers over her nipples until they were rock hard.

"Tug them," the deep smokey voice insisted.

Jennifer tugged at her nipples and could feel herself still trembling. She needed to climax desperately and being made to play with her own nipples was making the wetness between her legs run down between the cheeks of her backside.

"Harder," the older woman said in a very demanding tone.

Jennifer pulled and tugged at her nipples harder than she ever had and heard herself whimpering. She realised she had become a trembling mess and looked up to see her boss grinning at her.

"Hands on your head Jennifer," she ordered

Jennifer complied, and the older woman began squeezing and kneading the tender young breasts. As she pinched and tugged hard at the now extremely sensitive nipples, Jennifer heard herself whimpering louder and with a tone of anguished need.

"You want to orgasm Jennifer..." It was less a question and more a statement of fact.

Jennifer couldn't speak, but she nodded furiously.

The older woman chuckled a little devilishly.

"I like to see you like this, Jennifer. I will often make you feel like this. I will enjoy seeing you desperate, aching, wanting nothing more than to orgasm and prepared to do almost anything for it. But you belong to me now, my dear, and I will decide when you may orgasm and when you may not."

She tugged sharply on Jennifer's nipples and pinched them hard until Jennifer cried out.

"We will need to discuss a safe word for you Jennifer, so that you may stop me if things get too much for you. But not today. Today you won't need one. Today will just be some fun."

Jennifer could feel herself break into a sweat; she needed to climax so desperately she would do anything for release.

"I can see this is difficult for you Jennifer, but you are doing very well. Very well indeed. But you need to remember I choose where and when and how you orgasm from now on. If you defy me, there will be grave consequences. I am an enthusiastic fan of corporal punishment, Jennifer, so it is important for you to learn the rules and follow them. But we will discuss this all later with clearer heads. For now, just remember you belong to me totally, and you do nothing without permission. Do you understand, Jennifer?"

Jennifer nodded.

"Do you understand Jennifer?" The voice came more insistently and was accompanied by a sharp tug of her nipples.

Jennifer heard herself cry out and felt a flood of wetness between her legs. The sensation cleared her head enough for her to say, "Yes, Miss, I understand Miss."

The older woman gripped one nipple hard and twisted it.

"And what is it you understand Jennifer?" she asked in a warm, almost sweet tone while she twisted the nipple harder.

"I understand that I belong to you and I may not climax without permission," Jennifer managed to say.

Miss Carol relaxed her grip. "That's my good girl," she said and leant over to take the throbbing nipple into her warm wet mouth and sucked it gently.

Jennifer almost wept at the conflicting sensations.

The older woman then stood and said, "Seeing as it is a party and we have your new job to celebrate, I think I would like to see you orgasm today, Jennifer."

The younger woman's heart almost burst with anticipation at hearing those words.

"You may touch yourself for me, Jennifer, I want to watch you. Show me how you satisfy yourself."

Jennifer suddenly felt very self-conscious but slid her hand down between her legs and began to masturbate. She was unusually wet, and her clitoris was extremely sensitive, but it felt so good that she soon relaxed into a rhythm. Each time she remembered she was being watched a bolt of pleasure flashed through her and in less than the time it would usually take, Jennifer found herself on the verge of a climax.

An alarm went off in her head and she realised she had better check if she actually had permission. She was so close it was hard to speak, but she managed, "I'm close Miss, may I, Miss?"

Miss Carol smiled and said, "Yes Jennifer you may."

Jennifer closed her eyes and rubbed herself frantically and was finally rewarded with a powerful orgasm that spread from her clitoris to her whole body in wave after almost endless wave of satisfying pleasure. She slumped back on to the desk and was oblivious to anything around her until she heard her boss's deep smokey voice.

"You orgasm very quietly, Jennifer, but the expression on your face was sublime. I think I'd like to see that again."

Jennifer was only partly aware of what Miss Carol said, as she was comfortably sated. But she did feel her boss lean over the desk and open the drawer. Her ears prickcd up whcn shc hcard thc snap of the latex glove being put on, and she tried to work out what was going on. But before she could fathom anything she heard her name in that way she was growing to love.

"Spread your legs for me, Jennifer, I am going to make you orgasm again."

Jennifer felt a renewed surge of arousal pulse through her body. She had never had more than one orgasm so close together before. She wasn't even sure she could, but she was aching for her boss to do whatever she wanted with her, so she complied and spread her legs, exposing herself in a way she never had before. That sent a thrill through her that she couldn't describe, even to herself.

"Good girl," came the reward. "You are so beautiful my dear, and so wet. That makes me very happy."

Jennifer could feel her boss's fingers slipping and sliding around in between her wet swollen lips then suddenly, without warning she felt them plunge deep into her. She groaned involuntarily when she felt the increase in pressure like before and felt herself getting even wetter.

The older woman pressed her fingers deep inside Jennifer until she found the spot that made the young woman squirm and moan. She used her experienced fingers to tease the spot until her new acquisition began to tremble.

"Good girl... now touch yourself for me and make yourself orgasm with me inside you."

Jennifer reached down and began to rub herself. She was unsure if she could make herself climax again but as soon as she started, she could feel the deep pleasure inside her, throbbing and aching and connecting every part of her and she was suddenly sure she could. She rubbed hard and fast and could not resist the urge to thrust against her boss's fingers. Jennifer had never felt like that before. She was so hot she would have done anything she was asked.

She rubbed and thrusted and Miss Carol pressed deep into her until she was sure she was about to orgasm again. She opened her eyes and said, "May I Miss? Please may I?"

The pleasure in her boss's face was palpable as she grinned and said, "Yes, Jennifer you may. In fact, I insist."

Within seconds Jennifer felt a delicious wave of warmth and pleasure start from deep in her belly and spread out from there, gentle at first and then growing in intensity until she could hear herself moaning loudly as the pleasure reached its peak, suspending her there for one perfect moment before it finally subsided.

She was stunned at the strength of it. She had never experienced anything like that before. She never knew pleasure like that existed. She suddenly felt empty as her boss withdrew her fingers and left her laying on the desk panting and wondering if she would ever make sense of the world again.

"Well, that one sounded better my dear and your face looked just as good. Let's see how the next one goes."

Jennifer made a move to object but caught the look on her boss's face and realised that was a bad idea. Instead, she politely said, "I'm not sure I can, Miss. I've never -"

The older woman cut her off abruptly, "You can, and you will, Jennifer. It is not up to you at any rate. I would just love to turn you over and spank that glorious bottom until it is glowing red and then explore how tight you are back there as my Christmas gift to myself, but I don't think you're ready for that yet; so don't tempt me."

Jennifer said nothing at all, but the word 'yet' was ringing loudly in her head and sending thrilling shivers up and down her spine.

Miss Carol pressed Jennifer's thighs wide apart and smiled. "You look divine my sweet girl. I'm going to enjoy this."

She began gently playing and teasing and then began tugging at Jennifer's wet lips, pulling on her small triangle of hair and squeezing her mound hard, and within a brief time Jennifer was lost in the feeling of it all again and didn't care what happened to her, as long as the pleasure didn't stop. She felt her boss push inside her, and she moaned with delight. Her body and soul were lost to the sensation.

Miss Carol pressed deep inside with one hand but kept tugging and playing with Jennifer's most intimate parts with the other. She pressed hard on the area that had made Jennifer squirm and found it worked it's magic again. Within a minute or so Jennifer was moaning and bucking involuntarily against her boss's hand while her boss was pressing into her and roughly tugging at her clitoris.

Jennifer began to moan and whimper without really realising it. Her legs were trembling, and she broke into a sweat. She needed this. She needed it so bad.

"Play with your nipples, Jennifer." She heard the order, but it took her a moment to translate it and make her hands move. Once she did, she heard her reward: "Good girl."

Jennifer was a mess again. A whimpering, bucking, throbbing mess. She could make no sense of anything. She couldn't even tell what was being done to her or who was doing it. She heard herself starting to beg. She'd never begged for anything in her life, but she was begging now, and she didn't care.

"Please Miss, please don't stop. Please, I need it, please," She could hear herself saying.

She thought if she didn't climax soon she might die. She felt her new mistress pressing hard into her. Deep and hard and rubbing a thumb fiercely across her clitoris. Jennifer could feel her boss's other palm pressed down low and firm on her belly and she could hear herself begging which seemed to spur Miss Carol on.

"Keep playing with your nipples Jennifer, tug them harder. That's it, do it harder for me."

Jennifer heard the command and responded on autopilot. Any pretence of conscious thought had left the building. She was incapable of anything other than simply obeying her boss's command. She could feel a force building inside her, but she didn't know what it was. She pulled and tugged at her nipples and bucked uncontrollably against the fingers inside her but was held down by the strong hand pressing on her belly. She knew she was making sounds, but she had no idea if they were words or mindless grunts.

She thrusted and bucked and tugged, incapable of anything else.

She felt a heat building in her feet, in her head, in her belly, she couldn't tell where any more. It almost felt like somebody was pouring hot water over her skin. In her navel, over her belly, it was delicious, but she couldn't pinpoint it. She couldn't pinpoint anything. She could hear a voice, a voice she wanted to obey, so she strained to hear and tried to make sense of it.

"Yes, Jennifer, yes. Climax for me, go with it, take it. Orgasm for me now my dear, let it happen."

Jennifer struggled to understand what she was hearing. She tried to focus on something, anything. She could feel her mistress pushed up inside her and pressing down on her from the outside. She could feel her own hands tugging at her nipples and squeezing her breasts.

She could hear the voice, but it was too far away, and she couldn't get a hold of it. Then she felt her feet and she thought of her sexy red shoes, smiling because she knew then her life was going to be fantastic. She was going to be rich and successful, she was going to travel the world and have great sex, and she was never going to need a man again.

The heat in her feet shifted to her belly and became a glowing red ember. Jennifer concentrated on the glow and let it lead her closer to the voice. The voice she wanted to succumb to. She could hear it telling her to orgasm. Telling her to let go and take her pleasure, her release.

She knew she wanted it, she knew she had to comply, but she couldn't seem to get there.

She could feel the deep ecstasy of the pressure inside her, pushing against the pressure of the warm palm on her belly. She felt like her desire, her need, her whole self was being held and compressed between these two hands.

Jennifer realised her pleasure, her life, her all, was in her mistress's hands, and she knew she had to give in to that and let it be. It was like a flash of truth that lit up her mind for just long enough for her to let go of control and let herself be taken. Truly taken by another living being.

As Jennifer surrendered to her fate, the voice took on a commanding tone, ordering her to comply. She had no choice but to obey the voice. She let go of everything but the voice and gave herself into those hands. The glowing fire in her belly expanded beyond her and exploded into a thousand tiny sparks, and Jennifer exploded with it.

She felt herself shudder and convulse as the pleasure finally hit her like a meteor and she heard herself cry out. She felt the tiny embers rain down on her, extinguishing themselves on her skin and finally, she collapsed into the darkness that was left behind.

She laid on the desk, limp and spent, almost lifeless. She felt as if she was looking down at herself, tousled, dishevelled and totally sated. She was sure the neat line of roses on her stockings were dreadfully askew. She realised her shoes had come loose and were barely held on by her toes. She felt her boss remove the red shoes, saw her admired them for a moment, and then place them on the floor. Then Jennifer felt her stockings being rolled down and removed.

Miss Carol guided the spent and sleepy girl onto her feet, pulled her into her lap on the large leather recliner and pulled a blanket off the back of it and over them both. She brushed the hair off the young woman's face and kissed it softly.

Jennifer felt herself being held safe and warm. She felt gentle kisses on her forehead as she snuggled into the safe arms that held her and slept.

At some point, Jennifer woke up and tried to get her bearings. She heard a familiar, reassuring voice say, "Close your eyes little one, we are fine here until morning. Then I will take you to your new home, so you can start your brand-new life."

Jennifer saw the red shoes on the floor beside her discarded clothes, and she remembered where she was and how she got there. She smiled as she fell back to sleep secure in the knowledge that everything was going to be okay from now on.

*****

The Mermaid's Pearls

I was warming my favourite bar stool when they walked in. '*They*' were the hottest pair of red high heeled shoes I had ever seen. Don't get me wrong, I'm not usually the sort of guy that goes for the shoes and not the girl, if you know what I mean. I appreciate what they do for a shapely leg and a pert behind, and I love that special sway they give to a sexy walk, but given the choice between the shoe and the girl in it, I'm coming down on the side of the girl every time. Despite that, I did realise that it took me until they had sauntered confidently halfway across the room before I actually looked up the see who was wearing them.

I was expecting some super sophisticate or maybe even a high-class working girl, as my eyes worked their way slowly up the bare legs to the short black skirt, the white blouse with just enough buttons undone to reveal an enticing cleavage nestled in a red lace bra. But when I got to the face, I was surprised. This was a 'nice' girl.

A girl completely out of place in a dive like this. As I watched the rest of her progress towards the bar, I noticed that the shoes were walking confidently but the girl looked a little nervous as if she was just along for the ride.

She perched herself on the stool beside me and smiled. "Hi, I'm Andrea," she said with such a pretty smile it caught me by surprise. "Would you like to buy me a drink?"

"Sure," I replied, a little taken aback. "I'm Charlie, what would you like?"

"You choose," she said, "I don't mind."

I signalled to the barman. "One of whatever you think the lady might like please, George, and I'll have another while you're at it."

"Shall I put it on your tab, bro?" George said with a sarcastic wink.

In reality, I never paid for my drinks. George, my brother, was not only the barman and the manager but was a half owner of *The Mermaid's Pearls* the seedy little dockside pub that had been left to us by our uncle. Probably just to annoy our mother, which it did.

So yes, I owned the other half of the pub, but the deal was I was a silent partner – very silent. I had no desire to own or run the place, whereas George was in his element. So, he ran things however he wanted, and I kept quiet and tried not to drink all of the profits.

George brought the drinks.

"Is he actually your brother?" Andrea asked

"Sure is, George meet Andrea. Andrea, my brother George."

George put out his hand to shake hers. "Pleased to meet you, Andrea," he said.

"You don't look like brothers," she responded

"Yeah I know," George said. "I got the looks, junior got the brains."

Andrea laughed, and it sounded delightful.

Truth be told, George and I looked a lot alike, or at least we did when we were young. But his choice of sport had made all the difference over the years. While I was a swimming, tennis and beach volleyball kind of guy, big brother George was more your rugby and boxing type, so, numerous broken noses, a jaw reconstruction, and some very nasty ear injuries had left their mark, while I had largely been left unscathed.

George was also a lot more solid than I was. Not just physically but also in his nature. He was the kinda guy that was devoted to his kids, still got on well with his ex-wife and was happy to work all the hours God gave him behind the bar. Whereas I was the flighty baby brother. I didn't have any children, I changed university degrees three times before I decided to drop out and sell real estate, and all my exes would happily back over me in a car park if they had the opportunity. Fortunately, real estate was lucrative enough for me to make plenty of money without having to do much work, which was just the way I liked it.

Andrea smiled up at me. "So, I guess if your brother works here, you must come here often."

I laughed. "Well if we're going with the corny lines I guess the obvious question is, what's a nice girl like you doing in a place like this?"

"Well, I'm due to get married next week, and I just discovered my fiancé is cheating on me, so I've borrowed some clothes and shoes from the girl upstairs and come out to get drunk and get laid. I was kinda hoping you could help me with that," she said.

I must admit that I was speechless. I had never really had such a nice, pretty, intelligent looking girl come on to me so strongly. Part of me wanted to say 'no' and scnd her home safe, but I figured if it wasn't gunna be me then it would be somebody else. I looked around the bar, took stock of who was there, and remembered some of the tales that I'd heard from the working girls that sometimes came in here for shelter on a cold night. I decided that at least if I were the one, I would know that she was okay. Christ knows why she brought out the protective side in me. I'm not normally that kind of guy, but she just looked so helpless and innocent, and I didn't want her to get hurt.

"I'm sure I can help you with that, Andrea." I signalled George "Another drink for the lady please."

Andrea downed the last of the first drink and George brought the second which she started on with enthusiasm.

"Slow down, honey, slow down," I said "There's no need for you to be completely wasted. I like my lovers to at least be conscious."

She hit me with her beautiful high beam smile again and my heart almost melted.

"So, have you told him the wedding is off yet?"
I asked

"No," she said. "I'll still marry him. He is too
rich for me not to. But I'm not going to sit at
home having no fun like a *good girl* between now
and then. I intend to make sure that every part of
me is 'used goods' before the wedding and I'm
not signing his stupid prenup either. If he insists
I'll tell his mother it is all off because he is
bonking her hairdresser. That will put a cat
amongst the pigeons."

"So, you're serious then?" I asked

"Deadly serious," she replied, and for the first
time I saw just how determined she was.

"So," I said rather awkwardly, "Where were you
hoping for the action to take place?"

"I was hoping that you might have somewhere,"
she grinned. "But if I have one more of George's
delicious drinks I'll be happy for you to do me
here on the bar." I laughed to cover up my
discomfort with that thought, more than anything
else. I signalled to George for another round of
drinks then suggested we take them to
somewhere a bit more private. "George has an
office just at the back here sweetheart." I
motioned towards it. "Would you like to go out
there? It's a bit more private than the bar."

"Lead on," she said.

We stood in George's office, momentarily
awkward but then she took two confident steps
towards me in those mesmerising hot shoes and
without hesitation she kissed me. Her lips were
soft and warm and tasted of the sweet pink drink

George had made her. George's cocktails were always far too sweet for my taste. I'm more a bourbon guy. But on Andrea's lips the sweetness was divine. Her tongue ran across my lips, tentatively at first but then her confidence increased, and she was exploring my mouth, my tongue, and practically my throat as I began to return her kiss with the passion that was rising in me by the second.

I cupped the back of her head in my hand and pressed my tongue deep into her pretty mouth, feeling her moan in approval. I felt my dick start to swell in my pants as she pressed her body hard up against mine.

She began to undo my shirt buttons and run her fingers through the hair on my chest and circle her fingertips around my nipples.

My cock was straining eagerly against the inside of my pants, and I was as turned on as I ever remembered being. I had to have her, but I didn't want to rush this; it was far too good for that.

I turned us around and sat her on George's desk. She was unbuttoning her blouse in a second, and I reached around her to unclip her bra, granting freedom to the bounteous soft flesh it was holding.

I feasted my eyes on the sight of her milky white skin and erect nipples. I fell upon them like a starving man and took one nipple into my mouth and sucked hard. Andrea groaned, ran her fingers through my hair and said, "Harder, please suck it harder." I complied with her wishes and sucked until I was sure it would leave a mark, then I switched my attentions to the other nipple and sucked and licked and flicked it with my tongue until Andrea was panting.

I pushed her back, so she was lying on the desk and I moved my activity further south. I hitched her skirt up and nearly died at the realisation that she wasn't wearing underwear.

I spread her legs wide and plunged right into her, tongue first.

She was so wet I was having a total pussy juice facial in no time at all. She squirmed and bucked and rubbed herself on my face while I did my best to keep my lips and tongue working all the good bits.

"Put your fingers in me," she demanded between moans.

I slid first one, then two fingers deep into her pretty pussy then started licking her clit. She squealed in delight and began riding my face and my hand.

I was a bit out of practice, so I wasn't sure how long I could keep it up for, but I really wanted to please her which, I am almost embarrassed to say, was most out of character.

I needn't have worried about my staying power though because she soon cried out, "I'm gunna cum, dear god I'm gunna cum, Jesus fuck yes...."

She screamed and shuddered deeply before she collapsed onto the desk.

I figured I would give her a few minutes to catch her breath and then see if I was going to get properly lucky, now that she had got what she wanted. But she pulled me up to kiss her, hungrily licking her own juices off my face. I could have blown just at the thought of that, but I didn't, thank God.

"Fuck me now, Charlie," she said with a glimmer of a smile.

I didn't need to be asked twice. I undid my pants and had them off in a flash. I moved between her legs and pressed the head of my cock up against her. I'm not sure what possessed me, but I looked up into her eyes and asked, "Are you sure?"

"Yes. Charlie," she said. "Fuck me now."

With that, I felt a surge of lust and drove my cock hard into her. She was super tight but so wet and slippery she took it all with ease, right up to the hilt, and let out a deep animal groan.

I couldn't help myself, I was overwhelmed by a primal urge and started to fuck her harder and faster than I had managed since my teens. I was lost in the sounds of her, the tightness of her and the heat of her.

I'm no expert, but I was sure she was already building to another orgasm. She squealed and groaned and cried out, "I'm cumming! Jesus, I'm cumming!" She fell quiet for a moment after. I figured I could just go for it and finish, but for some reason, I held off for a while despite my balls aching to unload. She rested for just a moment or two then she lifted her legs so that they were running up my chest and said, "Come on Charlie, do me like you mean it."

I grabbed her thighs and began to fuck her like I was some sort of porn-star super-stud, she wrapped her ankles around my neck. I could feel those fucking sexy shoes on my face. I could smell the leather and just having them so close to me spurred me on to fuck like a warrior. I'm no expert, I normally only know a girl is cumming if she tells me, but I was sure Andrea climaxed several more times and finally reached down between her legs and began playing with her clit while I fucked the hell out of her.

She was making the hottest sounds once she began pleasuring herself like that. The sight of her, coupled with the smell of the leather and the feeling of tightness around my shaft meant that I couldn't help myself. As soon as Andrea began to cry out with another climax, I hit my limit and heard myself groaning like an animal as I pumped my hot jizz into her willing wet cunt.

We both stopped, panting, sweat covering our skin and I thought what a lucky guy I was that she picked me. It had been the best fuck I could remember, maybe the best ever.

Once she caught her breath, Andrea sat up, and I passed her what was left of her drink. She sipped it so sexily that I began to suspect my night might not be over. She finished about half the glass then slithered down onto her knees and took my limp dick into her mouth.

I was about to tell her it was a futile effort, when the warmth of her mouth and the magic movements of her tongue made me feel like I could manage another boner after all. She licked and sucked like an expert, reaching up to fondle my balls in the process. I looked down at her, kneeling at my feet in just a skirt and those sexy high heels and sure enough, my blood started to pump back into my cock. Soon she had me rock hard and raring to go.

I couldn't remember the last time a woman wanted me so badly that she came back for seconds, but Andrea stood up, turned around and leant over the desk. She lifted her skirt, exposing her ripe buttocks, looked back over her shoulder and said, "Come on Charlie, I want more."

I'm not always the sharpest tool in the shed, but she didn't have to say that twice. I slid my rock-hard cock into her with no hesitation and grabbed her hips. I gave it to her like I was trying to push her into next week and she met every thrust with eager cries of, "More Charlie! Harder! Fuck me, Charlie, fuck me hard! More I want more! More! More!"

I was beginning to fear I was not going to be enough for her. I had never seen a woman so hot, but I was driven to try to keep up.

I had been so absorbed in the fucking of this unbelievable creature that I hadn't heard the door open until I heard George's voice

"Need a hand there, little brother?" he asked

I don't know how long he'd been there, but it was long enough for him to have a massive erection. One thing I didn't mention before about the differences between my brother and me is the size of his cock. Mine is about average, but his is enormous.

His ex-wife used to say it took three natural births before she could stand the size of his dick in her and by then it was the only part of him she liked. It took a lot to get him hard, but once he was up, it was like a monster.

Andrea looked over at him and smiled. She signalled for him to come to her and within moments she had his cock in her mouth and mine still rammed up her cunt. George grinned at me. We hadn't tag-teamed a girl for over twenty years.

In hardly any time at all, I was beginning to download a second serving of steaming jizz into this incredible little hottie.

Then George said, "Time to swap ends, baby brother."

Andrea was all over it. She spun around and turned onto her back. For a moment I wasn't sure she could take all that my brother had to offer, but George spread her legs with his enormous hands and pressed the head of his giant cock just inside of her. He worked his way into her inch by inch until he was in up to his nuts. I guess my contribution to her juices might have helped a little, but I was still totally impressed by how such a nice tight, good girl could take an enormous cock like that.

Andrea hung her head over the edge of the desk and sucked me into her mouth again. I figured there was no harm in letting her, even though it was now down to George to satisfy her. He grinned at me as he fucked her while she sucked me, and before I knew it, I could feel life ebbing into my cock again. I hadn't been able to manage that sort of recovery since I was a teenager but sure enough I had a hard-on, and to my surprise and delight, Andrea was taking the whole lot into her mouth and down her throat.

I'd only ever had deep throat from a hooker before, and I had to pay extra for it. Here was this girl I just met, swallowing me down like it was nothing. I was overcome with admiration and quite jealous of the cheating bastard she was going to marry. I was so turned on I grabbed her head in my hands and began to fuck her throat like she was a hot porn starlet. George was watching the action, and it took him up a level. He began to really pound her with his massive cock.

Andrea was meeting George's every punishing thrust and still managing to give the head of my cock the best throat massage I would ever have in my life.

I was sure Andrea orgasmed several times, but either way the three of us were having the best night of fucking you could ever ask for.

I watched as George grabbed her ankles just above those shoes, lifted her legs and pulled them wide apart. I knew that move. It meant he was about to unleash the beast. He began to fuck that monster cock of his into Andrea's tight little snatch like a piston and she began to moan and tremble and whimper as best she could with a throat full of cock.

I was about to unload again and wasn't sure if I should do it down her throat, so I pulled out and blew all over her tits. A few shiny beads of cum sprayed in a line across her throat like the perfect pearl necklace and I smiled at the irony. It was what our pub was named after, in a sly sort of way.

As my cock subsided to practically nothing, I watch Andrea's cum soaked tits bouncing wildly as my brother let her have it. She was making the most amazing noises, and I could see her legs were trembling in George's hands. I reached out and grabbed both her nipples in my fingers, held them tight and let them tug as she was pounded. I could feel her squirming beneath my touch, and it made my balls ache even though they had already been emptied out about as much as I thought they possibly could be in one day.

"Oh, fuck yes. George! Don't stop!" she cried out. "I'm gunna cum again!"

I felt her tremble under my fingers and watched as her face contorted beautifully. She closed her eyes, and I thought she had finally had enough, but then she reached her arms up and somehow pulled herself up to hang on around George's neck. He let her ankles go, and she wrapped her legs around his waist as she begged him to keep fucking her.

I watched in delight as my horse of a brother was pile driving this pretty girl standing up and began to wonder if she would ever have enough. I could see the red shoes rubbing up and down George's back as Andrea bounced on his cock, leaving scratch marks on his skin, it looked so fucking hot I almost felt life in my cock again.

"Charlie?" Andrea said. "Charlie, where are you?"

I approached her from behind and said, "I'm here, baby, what do you need?"

"Can you get hard again?" she managed to ask between thrusts.

"Sorry," I said, "I think I'm all fucked out for the night."

"Your fingers then, Charlie, use your fingers please." She practically begged.

"Where do you want them, honey?" I asked. "You're already full of George."

"Put them up my arse Charlie, please fuck my arse with your fingers." She said

I was astounded; I have never had a woman ask for that. The only anal action I ever had was paid for and there was a surcharge for it.

"Now, Charlie, now." she demanded, "Put your fingers in my arse!"

I didn't have any trouble getting my fingers wet. Andrea's juices were flowing freely. I wasn't all that sure what I was doing, and Andrea was in motion, so I fumbled and took a while to press one finger up against her butt hole and push. At first I couldn't get in at all - she was obviously a virgin in that part of the world. Then as she thrust down on to George's cock she opened up and my finger began to slide in. It took a bit of effort and a few more thrusts but soon I had one finger right up her tight hot arse while she was moaning and going to town on it.

I could feel George's cock inside her, but I tried not to think about that. I just pushed up into her for all I was worth.

Without warning, I felt Andrea shudder and gasp and I wondered if she was having another orgasm, but that thought was soon overtaken by the animal sounds coming from my brother.

I knew those noises. He was about to fill Andrea up with his own load. He had hold of her hips and pounded his last few thrusts into her and then cried out like a wounded animal as he exploded into her hot, tight hole.

George's knees were a bit wobbly, so I slid my finger out of Andrea and moved out of the way as he took a step forward and rested her backside on his desk. He slid what was left of his monster erection out of her and Andrea dropped right to her knees, trying to give it mouth to mouth. I figured there was no resurrecting that monster again tonight.

I felt a little sorry for her and a bit like a failure. Between the two of us, we hadn't managed to satisfy one woman. But as I watched her kneeling there, licking her own sweet juices off my brother's cock with her ankles crossed behind her, showing off those red-hot shoes, I was thinking how lucky I was to have had her at all.

I began to replay the night's events over in my head and blow me down if I didn't feel a sign of life in my cock. I began stroking myself and sure enough, I was getting some blood down there. Andrea saw me and grinned. She motioned for me to come within arm's reach and she took over working my cock back to life. Before I knew it, I was hard and aching to fuck.

George laid Andrea across the desk and she grabbed me with her legs to drag me to her. I could feel those heels digging into my back and it spurred me on. I easily slid my newly hardened cock right into her steaming hot pussy. She moaned with what sounded like delight, looked up into my eyes, lifted her legs up onto my shoulders and flashed me that magic smile. "Come on Charlie, fuck my arse." She said.

I almost lost my load just at the sound of that, but she didn't have to ask twice. She wrapped her arms around her knees and pulled her legs up to give me easy access. My cock was nice and slick with her and George's mess when I pressed the head of it where I had just had my finger. It took some effort but soon she had taken the head into her incredibly tight hole and then I was able to work myself into her a bit at a time. I grabbed hold of her ankles and pushed her legs back further. Soon enough I was fucking her sweet, tight butt like we were old hands.

I looked over and realised she was sucking George's cock and I thought that would be a futile exercise, but then I realised she had managed to get him hard again. I couldn't believe it, I thought that would be impossible, but there she was giving him the hottest blow job I had ever seen.

She grabbed at George's hands and pushed them down to her pussy, and he began fingering her with one hand and playing with her clit with the other all the while sliding his massive monster cock further and further into her mouth until it had to have been going down her throat.

I was amazed. George had often complained that no woman could deep throat him, not even his favourite hooker, and yet Andrea was managing it without so much as a blink.

She was so fucking hot I thought we were all going to explode.

George was fingering her deep and hard while I was pounding her arse more furiously than I could have imagined possible. All of a sudden George cried out and began to shudder. He was obviously unloading right down Andrea's throat. I almost blew my own load at the thought but all of a sudden I could smell the leather of the shoes, and it brought me back to the job at hand.

Andrea emptied her mouth of George's fast-shrinking cock and demanded, "More Charlie, more! Harder, yes George, don't stop please, deeper, more! Don't stop, don't stop, don't stop!" She was screaming, and I was sure I could hear the bar patrons cheering us on from outside the - thankfully - locked door.

I had hold of her ankles and was fucking her with all I had. George was working her pussy with his fingers, and I prayed we would get her to where she needed to be soon.

Suddenly, I felt her arse tighten around my cock and she shuddered so hard all three of us felt it in our bones.

She went stiff, and silent and arched her back and then screamed like a banshee.

I hoped to God she was done because I had started to cum up her tight arse and I knew that when I was done, I was not going to even contemplate getting hard again for a month. George was also done and dusted, and I certainly didn't want to let any of the rabble at the door anywhere near her.

Andrea slumped down on the desk, limp like a rag doll and panted.

Once my cock stopped twitching, I slid out of her arse and let her legs down slowly.

She looked up at us with a wide grin and glassy eyes. The gorgeous red shoes fell to the floor one at a time with a surprising thud. Andrea smiled and said, "Thank you, boys."

She seemed like a tiny doll as George lifted her onto the sofa in his office and covered her with a blanket. She was asleep almost instantly. George, ever the gentleman, left her a note with the number of a trustworthy taxi driver that would get her home safe and said she could put it on the pub's tab. Then we turned off the light. George went back to the bar and I headed home.

In the morning she was gone. There were two kisses and a big smile drawn on the note. The red shoes were still there where they had fallen.

George hung them on a hook behind the bar in case she came back for them, but she never did.

About a week later I saw a newspaper article about some super rich dude and his gorgeous young bride.

She looked radiant, and I smiled.

*****

Aladdin's Cave

"Girl, those shoes are hot! You look so damn good I would do you myself if I could afford you," Melinda said as I approached our usual corner for the night.

"If things are too slow tonight, I'd consider giving you a freebie just to keep warm," I responded, accepting the greeting hug and air kisses.

"You give it away too often already, honey. You'll never get off this corner 'til you stop with the freebies." Melinda chided for about the millionth time.

"So, you're telling me that I'm still working street corners at my age because I'm too kind-hearted?" I scoffed. "So, what's your excuse?"

"It's my love of the outdoors that keeps me on the streets," she said.

We laughed too much at that, as we always did.

"Freebies can be useful," I said. "I gave George a freebie earlier today and he let me have these shoes." I did a little spin to show off my acquisition. They were by far the best shoes I'd ever even touched, let alone owned. They were a tiny bit scuffed and showing some wear but heck, so was I.

George owned the local pub, *The Mermaid's Pearls*, and Melinda was forever teasing me about being sweet on him.

"I knew I'd seen those heels before," Melinda laughed. "That's the pair that's been hanging behind the bar at *The Mermaid*.

"Yep, that's them. I've been eyeing them off for ages, and today George surrendered and gave them to me," I bragged

"I ain't even gunna ask what you did to deserve them, but whatever it was, it was worth it. You look hot as fuck."

It was an unlikely friendship, Melinda and me. She was young, working to support her boyfriend and a habit. I was older and had been in the business too long. Far too long. When I started out, I thought I'd do it just to pay my way through uni. But then it turned out to be easy money and I couldn't get away. Trouble is, money that comes easy seems to go just as easy. So, before I knew it, I was an old girl working the streets most nights just to make ends meet.

I had a plan, but it never seemed any closer to fruition. I had inherited a small cottage just on the edge of town from an old Aunt, but it needed some work to be habitable. New wiring, plumbing, that sort of thing. If I could just get a few thousand dollars together I could fix it up, stop renting a flat, and maybe even retire. Or semi-retire.

I thought I'd like to keep one or two regulars but see them in the comfort of my own home rather than hanging about on street corners, barely dressed, waiting for cars to pull up and hoping their heaters were working.

"Ay up," Melinda said as a black limousine slowed down to cruise past us. We both struck our 'available' pose, but the limo kept going. No real surprise. Those sorts rarely stopped for girls like us. We watched it drive slowly down the street, passing several other hopefuls. But still not stopping.

"Dang," Melinda said. "I bet their heater works just fine!"

We both laughed too much, again.

We went back to idle chat until we saw the limo pull around the corner. It had obviously gone around the block. We posed and again it cruised past, only much slower as if they were trying to get a better look. Melinda and I worked it as best we could but to no avail.

"Ass hat," Melinda said to the rear bumper in the distance. She was looking tired and a bit pale tonight.

I figured she would like a couple of early ones so that she could head home, so when I saw the limo pull around the corner again I said, "Work it, girl. They're back for another look."

Melinda went to the curb and did her utmost to get their attention. I stood just behind her, available but not actually hopeful, despite feeling unusually confident and sexy in my new red shoes and almost matching frock.

It was a wraparound dress from the local op shop that would have been the height of fashion at some point deep in the past. But what the heck, it granted easy access to the important areas and didn't mess up my hair getting it on and off in the back of cars.

The limousine slowed to a stop right in front of us, and the passenger window slid down. The sound of throbbing music wafted out with the distinctive smell of weed.

'*Bucks night or graduation party*,' I thought to myself and decided Melinda would be more their type, so I went to step back but my feet didn't want to move. In fact, seemingly on their own, my feet moved to stand me right beside Melinda, making it obvious I was quite available.

Once I got closer, I could see the guy in the passenger seat was no kid. He was a swarthy kind of guy probably in his thirties and not bad looking.

"Looking for whore," he said in a very thick accent.

"Well you've come to the right place, honey," Melinda said pushing herself just a little in front of me. I tried to back off and let her have this one, but my feet had other ideas and held their ground.

The guy seemed to be conferring with someone in the back, then I heard another deeper, accented voice in the background say, "*The red shoes*."

A thrill ran through my whole body from my toes up, and I was suddenly sure tonight was going to be worth it.

The back door opened. Music and smoke came tumbling out of what looked like a mobile disco. There were flashing coloured lights dancing in the darkness like giant fireflies and I could make out the shape of multiple dark, sexy looking men smoking from a hookah.

My brain was telling me to back away and let Melinda take this one, but my feet stepped right on into the limo and took me with them. Several hands guided me to a seat. The music was loud and unusual, and the lights made it difficult to see how many men there were; for a moment I felt a sense of panic and wanted to get back out, but the door was shut and we were moving so there was no escape. Once I'd accepted that I felt an odd sense of calm confidence flood up from my feet and I was sure I could handle whatever was about to happen.

One guy tapped me on the shoulder and started making hand gestures. He rubbed his middle finger and thumb together which I took to be the universal sign for cash. Then he made gestures that I took to mean hand job and blow job. It dawned on me that he was negotiating a price, so I tried to ask how many men, but the music and the lights and the language barrier were making it difficult. I thought I could see five guys in the back of the limo with me, so I held up five fingers and sort of shrugged, asking if I was to do them all.

A barrage of laughter drowned out the music for a moment as if I'd made a funny joke. I tried to signal my usual price for those services, but I had no idea if I was understood.

I gave up. I figured the car was warm and whatever money I ended up with would be a bonus. Sitting just across from me was one guy that looked older than the others, maybe late forties or fifties. His fingers were littered with fancy gold rings, and he was smoking lazily from the ornate water pipe. He saw me checking him out and he smiled broadly. His teeth were almost all gold and when the lights flashed on him I was sure I saw diamonds in there too.

His mouth looked like Aladdin's cave. He offered me the pipe. I put my hand up to decline. He offered more insistently and said what sounded like, "Hashish, very good." I declined again. I was never much of a drink and drugs girl, especially on the job. I preferred to work with a clear head. He started speaking to the other men in a language I didn't recognise, but from the sound of his voice I decided he was the one who chose '*the red shoes*.'

He was pointing at guys and then at me and I could hear him a little over the music but didn't understand. Next thing I knew I had a guy on each side of me eagerly undoing their pants. I instantly felt more comfortable. We were getting down to the stuff I understood.

Soon I had an eager hard-on in each hand and felt like the night was going to turn out fine. As each of the first two guys got to their happy ending, they were replaced by other eager men with their pants down. This was beginning to feel like easy money, although I had no idea how much money we had agreed on.

There seemed to be a procession of stiff dicks to deal with, but I was relaxed and comfortable, so it was all good. After the second two guys got to their money shots, I had another one hunch in front of me with his erection in his hand, obviously wanting to put it in my mouth. We rearranged ourselves a bit and soon I had a nice mouthful as well as two hands full of stiff dick.

I don't often truly enjoy my work, but I was feeling pretty good and even a bit aroused by the scenario as one by one I satisfied the whole limo full of guys, one way or another. All the while the older guy sat and watched and smoked his pipe. Each time I looked in his direction and the lights shone the right way I could see the flickering shimmer of his teeth, so I knew he was grinning.

When the steady stream of eager cocks was exhausted, I figured my work was done. When I looked up the older guy was still grinning, but it wasn't until he made a beckoning motion with his fingers and pointed to his crotch that I noticed he had undone his pants and was stroking a raging hard-on.

He motioned for me to come to him. I figured one more wasn't going to hurt and there was something about this guy I found strangely appealing, So I dropped to my knees in front of him and took his cock straight into my mouth.

He put his hands on my head, something I don't usually allow with a first-time client, so I took my mouth off his cock and shook my head. "No," I said

He laughed and ran a finger down my face. He rubbed his finger and thumb together signifying cash and said what sounded like, "Be good girl, I pay plenty, pretty red whore."

I figured, *why not*? If he meant to do me harm I was in trouble anyway, so I may as well get the most money I could out of this encounter.

I took his cock back into my mouth and I felt him groan. I ran my tongue around the smooth head. It felt really good. As I said, I don't often enjoy the actual work and I rarely if ever get aroused any more, but the feel of his hardness in my mouth and his hands on my head was making me horny.

I gave him the sort of head I normally reserve for a lover rather than a client. I was enjoying it as much as he was and almost wished I was wearing knickers as my wetness began to run down my thighs.

His hands were strong, but he mostly just fondled my hair; even when he was getting close to orgasm he didn't push, just held my head steady. I was so turned on when he finally climaxed that I automatically swallowed every drop. When he was done, he dragged me up into his lap and said, "Good, pretty whore."

He pulled the top of my dress open, grabbed my breast and began to fondle it. I would normally have stopped him doing things we hadn't negotiated but I was really turned on, and he wasn't hurting me, so I let him play with my tits and make my nipples hard while I laid back and enjoyed the attention.

I looked down and watched his bejewelled fingers pinching and flicking my hard nipple, mesmerised by the sight. He was watching me, and he pointed to one of the rings, nodding.

I figured he was asking me if I liked them, so I nodded back. He grinned widely and took one ring off his pinky put it on my index finger and laughed.

I had no idea what was going on, but I didn't mind. I was comfortable and felt safe and warm so if the ring was for me to keep, all the better. It was probably fake but even if it wasn't worth much, it was better than nothing.

I expected him to go back to my breasts after that little scene and when he didn't, I was a bit disappointed but not for long.

He ran his hand up my thigh directly to where I was wetter than I had been in a long time and began to play with my very horny pussy.

Clients rarely touched me like that and it felt great. He was firm but gentle and obviously knew his way around. In a matter of minutes, he had me panting and so close to cumming I would have begged him not to stop if I thought he would understand me. I caught a flash of an almost maniacal grin as I squirmed on his lap and prayed to the God of all things sexy that he was not going to leave me half done.

I could feel all the rings on his hand as he fingered and teased me, and I had a sudden flashback to a madam I once knew telling me there was *a fortune between those thighs* and I grinned to myself.

I could feel myself getting to the point of no return and I knew I was making a lot of noise, but it was lost in the music, or at least I hoped it was.

The client just kept going, I was sure he knew exactly what he was doing to me, and the thought of that was all I needed to push me over the edge into the best orgasm I'd had since I couldn't remember.

He knew, he was one of those rare guys that could tell, and he backed off what he was doing just at the right time so that I didn't have to push his hand away.

I laid there across his lap, panting and feeling pretty darn good for I don't know how long. I assumed we were done so I would be paid and dropped back to my corner now, but the older guy leaned forward and said into my ear, "Come to party pretty red whore."

I wasn't sure if it was a question, but I needed to get back to work. I had no idea how long I'd been in this limo but if my work was done, I needed to get paid and get back to the rest of the night.

I made the sign for cash to let him know I wanted to be paid now and then said loudly, "I need to get back."

I do know that increased volume doesn't make it easier to understand a foreign language, but I needed to be heard over the music.

The limo burst into laughter again, and I began to wish I had sorted out the money issue and insisted on payment up front as I usually would.

The older guy stroked my face very paternally and said, "Be good girl." He rubbed his fingers together. "Plenty, plenty."

I struggled against him and tried to get up. It was hard to negotiate in that position, but the lights flashed on my gorgeous new shoes and for some reason, I decided to just chill and go with the flow. I already had what I hoped was a gold ring. I was feeling very satisfied, so I figured it could do no harm.

I relaxed and nodded, and he grinned very widely and called out something to the guy in the front. I felt the car do a sharp turn and had to hold on to the older guy so as to not fall onto the floor. He grinned at me and said, "Pretty red whore."

I had no real sense of time in the darkness of the back of the limo with the lights flashing and the music pumping and all the 'happy smoke' in the air, but it didn't seem long before I was being ushered into a fancy hotel I didn't recognise. The concierge didn't seem at all phased by a group of men taking a scantily clad, and dishevelled woman up to their room. I guess it happens even in the best of places.

When we got out of the elevator, I was expecting a hallway, but we alighted directly into an elegant and sumptuously furnished room. I say room, but it was bigger than some entire houses I'd lived in. The older guy led me to the middle of a slightly smaller room to the side. A bedroom, no surprise. I thought he was making for the bed but instead he stood me in the middle of the room and undid my dress. It didn't take much, it was all held on with one tied belt, so I very quickly found myself standing naked in a room that was filling up with cheering men.

I felt a moment of panic rise in me, but I caught my reflection in a convenient mirror and saw how hot I looked standing there, naked but for those hot red shoes, and I suddenly felt like I could handle anything.

The older guy stood behind me and started fondling my tits. He gestured for the other men to come over closer and soon I had hands and tongues all over me. I had two guys sucking on my breasts and at least one between my legs licking my aching wet pussy, with other mouths and hands everywhere. Rather than being afraid I was as turned on as hell and felt like I was in heaven.

I leaned back into the arms of the older guy and felt safe. He reached down and began to expertly finger me until my legs were trembling so much I could barely stand. He gripped me tight around my waist as he could feel I was close to cumming and held me there as I shuddered and groaned my way through my second orgasm of the night.

As soon as I was done, it seemed as if there was a collective consciousness that lifted me up and put me on the high bed.

The groping continued. There was no part of me that wasn't being licked, sucked, or fondled. I had fingers and tongues all over me and I loved it. I had no idea how many men there were in the hotel room, but there seemed to be a constant stream of guys touching and teasing me.

Then a cheer went up and I heard the pop of a champagne cork. As a guy came toward me with the bottle, I felt nervous, but the older guy was at my head and said, "Plenty." As he rubbed his fingers together then took off another ring and put it on me.

I was so damn hot and horny and sure that the gold would be worth something that I nodded, and the cheer went up again. Two guys grabbed my legs and held them up while another guy pressed the neck of the champagne bottle into my pussy. I almost orgasmed on the spot, because it felt so good.

The guy with the bottle slid it in and out of me a few times then tipped it up, emptying champagne into my hot wet hole. When he pulled it out, there was a rush of eager mouths between my legs to drink as much of it as they could. Some were then spitting it into my mouth. The process was repeated again and again until the bottle was empty, then they brought another. I'm not much of a drinker, so the champagne was going to my head quickly, but the whole situation was so hot and felt so good I made no move to stop them.

I have no idea how many bottles they went through but by the end, I was drunk, horny as hell, and had cum so many times I lost count.

My older guy was at my head again, but I was struggling to understand what he was saying. "Fuck my pretty red whore," was what I thought I heard.

I tried to make bleary eye contact and say, "More money for that," rubbing my fingers together like he had, but I had no idea if he understood.

Next thing I knew I had a rock-hard cock in my pussy, another smooth hard cock in my mouth, tongues on my nipples, hands everywhere, and I was on top of the world. I felt so hot, so horny, and so wet I just laid back and enjoyed the attention. I orgasmed over and over as cock after cock exploded into both ends of me and over my tits and in my hands. I had always been afraid of a full-on gang bang, but this was the hottest thing I'd ever done, free or paid, and I was loving every thrusting, groaning, sweaty minute of it. I would have done it for free, but I shut up about that. I wasn't that drunk.

The endless stream of hot cocks, probing fingers and tongues, and the throbbing, aching need inside me for more, seemed to go on and on and on....

As the activity ebbed, my older guy was at my head again. He took a gold chain from around his neck and put it around mine. Then he moved away into the fog in my head and was lost. Next time I saw him, he was holding my ankles in his hands, kissing my hot red shoes then spreading my legs as wide apart as they could go.

He rubbed the smooth hard head of his cock against my clit until I moaned, then he slipped his full length deep into my throbbing wet pussy. A deep groan escaped my lips. He felt so good inside me. He held my legs up against his chest, and I hooked my hot red shoes around his neck. He grabbed the flesh of my thighs in a powerful grip and began to fuck me harder and faster than any of the young guys had managed.

My head was a whirl of pure ecstasy I had never felt before. Looking up at those sexy shoes as this strong man pumped his rock-solid cock into me like there was no tomorrow was like a dream come true. A dream I hadn't even known I'd had. But I knew I wanted it now; more than anything I wanted this guy to fuck me into next week.

I closed my eyes as the intensity of sensations grew in me until I thought I would expire. Again and again he made me cum and over and over again I wanted more. He seemed to be lasting forever, and I was wanting him to just keep going. I could hear myself moaning and whimpering and finally begging him to make me cum more, even if he didn't understand what I was saying. My legs were trembling up against his chest and we were both sweating and shaking.

Finally, I heard him cry out like a wounded old bull and grip the flesh of my thighs tight enough to bruise as he began to shudder and shake. I could feel his cock spewing his hot cum into me with an intensity I'd never felt in a guy before.

He collapsed down onto the bed beside me and called out something I didn't understand. A whole bunch of guys were suddenly upon me. Sucking on my nipples, taking turns to try to finger me to orgasm. Many of them succeeded in that task, with the older guy giving what sounded like instructions all the while.

I lost all track of time and space and became incapable of thinking or feeling anything but an urgent need to be touched and to cum over and over and over.

I heard my older man saying something that brought me back to myself: "Fuck you ass now, pretty red whore."

I'd done plenty of anal in my time but not with so many guys and I charged much more for it.

I tried to signal to him that it was more money. He nodded and grinned but I had no idea if he understood. He just took another gold chain from around his neck and put it over my head. I looked down at myself, naked, not a pretty young thing anymore. I caught sight of my hot shoes and thought, '*Oh fuck it, what have I got to lose?*'

I nodded. He grinned and said something to the younger men who lifted me up and flipped me onto my stomach. My feet only just touched the floor courtesy of my remarkably high heels. I felt somebody part my butt cheeks and then smear my back door with what I assumed was cold lube. That was a relief at least.

I heard my older guy whispering in my ear, "I fuck you ass now, pretty whore." Then I felt the head of his cock press against my hole. I did all I could to relax and take him and without much hesitation, I felt his cock being swallowed eagerly into my tight arse.

I didn't usually enjoy anal, but it was a good money spinner, so I did it from time to time, but this guy's cock felt so good up my arse that I nearly wept with pleasure. He fucked me slow and deep and hard, and it felt amazing. My head was a totally fogged up whirl of pleasure and disordered thoughts and I was lost in the ecstasy of it.

I heard him grunting behind me and giving instructions, but it was like the voice on a crossed phone line. I could hear it, but it didn't involve me at all. I felt my pleasure increase as fingers pushed up into my pussy and somebody started playing with my clit at the same time.

My older guy grabbed my hips so hard I knew I would have handprints on me for weeks, and began to fuck me like there was no tomorrow.

At about that point I was totally lost to reality. My memories of the rest of the night are hazy at best, but from what I recall the older guy fucked me into total oblivion. Building me up to an orgasm like I had never known before. It shattered through me like an earthquake and left me completely senseless. Unable to speak or think or move or do anything but just 'be' pleasure. Pure pleasure. I remember the sound he made as his own orgasm hit him and he unleashed his cum in my tight hot arse, grunting and groaning and crying out like a wild animal.

The rest of the night was a blur. Maybe the champagne douche caught up with me. Maybe spending all that time in a smoke-filled limo finally got to me. Maybe the giant mother of all orgasms simply scrambled my brain. Whatever the reason, the rest of the night was a shadowy montage of sweaty sex of every sort you can think of, with God knows how many men in God knows how many ways. I have no idea. All I know is I loved it, I wanted it, and I never felt so good.

When I opened my eyes the next morning everything hurt, even my eyelashes had a headache, and I was not sure where I was or what day it was or even who I was for sure.

It took me a while to blearily look around the room and get my bearings. I appeared to be in my flat. I laid my head back down and tried hard to fathom what the hell had happened.

I remembered the limo and then the party and realised that would explain why I was so sore. I had to struggle to work out how I got home. It took me a while but somewhere in the fog, there was the memory of somebody asking me my address and ushering me into the back of a taxi or a limo or maybe even a bloody flying saucer for all I knew. I only hoped I had managed to get dressed before the drive.

I opened my eyes again and tried to sit up, but the room spun out of control, so I stopped. I tried to just move my eyes but even my eyeballs hurt.

I could make out my red dress sort of draped over me, askew. So, I guessed I had been partially dressed for the trip home. I had a sudden feeling of dread, wondering if I had been paid, but then I figured it was such a great night I could write it off as a good night out if I hadn't managed to collect in the end.

I ran my hands over my eyes and tried to wake up and felt cold hard metal across my face. I looked at my hands through my bleary eyes and saw all my fingers were festooned with gold and diamond rings.

"Well darn," I said - or something a bit less polite. "Looks like I scored after all."

I tried to sit up again and felt a deep discomfort in my pussy. No surprise there, really. I reached down to see if I could detect any actual damage and felt something hard. I grabbed it and pulled, and a gold chain started to slide out from between my sore swollen lips bringing with it an assortment of rings, chains, and other jewels.

I nearly fainted at the sight, and the feeling of relief as my haul of treasures emptied out of me. It was sufficient to wake me up enough to do a proper scan of myself. By the time I had finished, I had a pile of gold and jewels from my hands and around my neck, wrists and ankles and from just about every orifice you can think off. That woke me up and I looked around the room to see my red shoes beside my bed, stuffed full of money. There were also several enormous wads of cash on my bedside table, on my bed and tucked into the belt of my dress.

"Holy fucking Jesus." I said as I collected up as much of the stash as I could find and put it in a pile on the bed.

I was gobsmacked and almost afraid the cops would be around any minute to arrest me for theft. I picked up my shoes, emptied the cash into the pile and found a hand-written note in badly spelled English but very ornate handwriting.

"Plenty, plenty for good girl. Pretty red whore." Was what I deciphered.

I sat on the edge of my bed and wept. I then wept in the shower, wept as I forced myself to eat some breakfast, wept as I took a bucket load of aspirin, and wept as I counted the cash and tried to decide on the best course of action. Even greatly hungover I knew this was my chance to set myself up comfortably for the rest of my life. I planned out the best course of action in my aching head and, once I was feeling well again, I put the wheels in motion.

I never went back to the corner.

The cash alone was enough to set me up completely in my old Aunt's house, with new wiring, new plumbing, a coat of paint, nice furniture, and a whiz-bang computer with a snazzy web cam.

Once cleaned up and appraised the jewellery was worth about five times as much as the cash, so I sold some of it and put the better pieces away for a rainy day.

Now I live a comfortable life in my cosy home with a couple of regular clients and some webcam work, just to pay the regular bills, but I am largely retired. All thanks to those hot red shoes.

My Aunt always had a horseshoe hanging above the front door for luck and nowadays, just above it, there hangs a pair of also retired, slightly scuffed and tattered but still damn sexy, hot red shoes.

George from the Mermaid put them up for me.

*****

Sadly, you've come to the end of this book. We hope you enjoyed it. Please consider visiting www.wolfstone.com.au and joining our mailing list so we can keep you up to date with all our latest stories as well as news and special offers for our fans.

We'd love to hear from you. Please tell us what you like, and we will give you more of it. You can contact any of us via our contact page. or our social media links on our website, wolfstone.com.au

Please keep in touch; we miss you already xx

*****